Skate to a Mountain Song

Skate to a Mountain Song

BY ALBERTA EISEMAN
AND INGRID SLADKUS

The Macmillan Company, New York

The Macmillan Company, New York
Collier-Macmillan Canada, Ltd., Toronto, Ontario
Library of Congress catalog card number: 66-11577
Printed in the United States of America

First Printing

Skate to a
Mountain
Song

Chapter One

Barbara looked over the books in her locker and chose what she would need for homework that night. She reached for the little plaid suitcase that held her skates, then, with her free hand, she tried to snap shut the combination lock. It wouldn't respond. Impatiently, she put books and skates on the floor and pressed the lock in with both hands.

By now the doors to the locker room were swinging open and high-pitched, laughing voices greeted the end of the school day.

Here comes the horde, Barbara thought. That means I'm late. I should have been on the street five minutes ago, waiting for Mother to drive by.

She recognized the voice coming from the locker directly behind her own.

"What are you going to wear Saturday night? Will it be a big party?"

"Not as big as the last one. Just our gang," her classmate Betty Jane answered. "Mom thought we were too hard on the house last month. I bought a new dress yester-day. . . ."

Barbara missed the description of the dress as she pushed past the next crowd of girls to enter from the hall. It had been months since BJ had asked her to one of her parties, she thought as she flew down the gray stone steps of Miss Farmer's School. She had refused one invitation, and BJ hadn't tried again. She had tried to explain that skating practice didn't leave her much free time, Barbara remembered, but she didn't really expect BJ to understand about that. Most girls didn't seem to.

Oh, well, so what, she told herself. It's not as if I had much in common with that crowd.

She waved to her mother, who had just pulled up to the curb.

"To the rink, please, James," she said with mock stuffiness and settled back in her seat.

"How was your Latin test, dear? As hard as you expected?" Mrs. McAllister asked as she drove her daily route across Central Park toward the West Side of New York.

"It certainly was," Barbara replied. "I would have done better if I had skipped my early skating session this morning. I mentioned it to Vittorio, but he seemed annoyed so I decided to take a chance. I really could have used those two extra hours of studying, though."

Her mother stopped for a red light on Ninth Avenue. She was a pretty, dark-eyed woman, with a few gray streaks in her black hair.

"You shouldn't have worried about Vittorio, Barbie," she smiled, looking for a moment very much like her daughter. "He's been your coach long enough to know

2

that even skating has to give once in a while when it comes to schoolwork."

They turned into Fiftieth Street, where Madison Square Garden is located.

"Madame Novotna called this morning," Mrs. McAllister said as she parked near the side entrance to the building. "Your new costume is ready, so I may as well pick it up right now. You go on up ahead, and I'll join you in about an hour."

Barbara started out of the car, then remembered.

"Oh, Mother, will you check on Marie's costume too? She was supposed to stop in for a fitting before leaving for Europe, but she didn't have a chance. Would you remind Madame Novotna that she'll need the outfit as soon as she comes back from the championships?"

Her mother nodded and drove away. As Barbara walked in under the marquee lettered ICELAND, her thoughts were with her friend Marie Whitman and the other members of the United States Figure Skating team now on their way to Europe to the World Championships.

She noted that the elevator was not on the ground floor and started up the stairs two at a time, her thick brown hair bouncing on her back. As she came into the dressing room, Barbara had already begun to unzip her little suitcase.

Vaguely she wondered why no one else was around. She reached for a hanger on which to place her cotton skirt, then, from her bag, she took beige tights and a yellow skating skirt her mother had knitted during the winter. A cardigan would keep her comfortable the first few minutes on the ice while she got accustomed to the contrast beween

3

New York's June weather and the perpetual winter of the rink.

Most time-consuming was the ritual of putting on her skates. While she methodically checked the laces at each eye, making sure they were extra tight around the instep and ankle, she missed the exchange of news and gossip that usually filled the room before the beginning of the afternoon session.

Absently, she checked her watch. No, she wasn't more than a few minutes later than usual. She slipped on her skate guards, then stood up before the mirror tying her hair back into a pony tail. She gave her reflection a quick once-over, making a face at the highly developed muscles of her legs. It was the price one had to pay for being a fine skater, that she knew, yet once in a while she wished her legs were as slim as the rest of her.

Impatient to start practicing, she hurried to the elevator, pulling on her white cotton gloves.

The usually loquacious elevatorman appeared lost in a study of the floor-indicator panel, and something about the frown on his face kept her from starting up their customary banter. The door slid open directly outside the rink, and she stepped onto the ridged-rubber floor covering.

Immediately feeling the drop in temperature, she buttoned up her cardigan. A Viennese waltz came over the loudspeaker, yet very few people were on the ice. Fewer than usual, she thought.

Barbara saw her coach, Vittorio Bianchi, leaning on the rail, majestically drawing on his cigar. With his immaculate blue blazer and tailored gray slacks, he looked every inch

4

the European gentleman. He raised a hand in greeting, all the while watching Jeff Byrnes attempt a difficult spin. Jeff lost his balance and fell, got up again and stamped his foot in anger.

Why, Vittorio didn't even seem to see him fall, Barbara thought, amazed at the lack of expression on his long, thin face. How most unlike him. She walked over to a bench and sat down next to Jeff's mother. Mrs. Byrnes looked up briefly from the intricate Norwegian sweater she was knitting, and it seemed to Barbara that her eyes looked red.

She bent down to remove her skate guards. As she put them on the bench, her eye caught a headline on the newspaper lying there.

She looked again, unbelieving. BRUSSELS CRASH KILLS 73 ON NY JET. Not our plane, surely not our plane, Barbara thought frantically. She looked up at Mrs. Byrnes, then down again at the paper, trying to reassure herself that she had been wrong. AIR CRASH KILLS 18 US SKATERS, the headline continued.

As in a nightmare, she sensed that the music had stopped. A weird silence enveloped the rink. In the center of the ice, the young skaters stood in a ragged line, their heads bent back, eyes focused upward toward the balcony coffee shop which overlooked the rink.

Barbara stepped onto the ice and skated noiselessly in their direction. Through the glass enclosure of the coffee shop the television set was clearly visible. No sound could be heard, but there was no misunderstanding the pictures of the smoking wreckage of a large jet plane lying among blackened, broken trees. An announcer followed and spoke

5

at some length. Still, no one made a move toward going up-stairs, closer to the television set.

They all stood hypnotized, knowing instinctively that the words the announcer was speaking were the names of their friends and competitors, the finest athletes in Ameri-can skating.

Chapter Two

Never, Barbara was sure, never in all her life would she forget that day. Someone upstairs switched off the television, and the skaters went back to practicing their routines, in complete silence. Barbara didn't feel like skating, but what else was there to do? She couldn't possibly talk to anyone.

Automatically, she skated several threes-to-center, as always in warming up. Anxious to avoid the faces of other skaters, she kept her eyes fixed on the position of her white-gloved hands.

She felt a sympathetic touch on her shoulder and turned to see an exceedingly thin, blond young woman skate past her rather awkwardly. It was Jean O'Day, a fashion model who had come to Iceland to be photographed for *Vogue* and had become a skating enthusiast.

How can Jean know how we feel, Barbara thought angrily. She hardly knew these kids. She has no idea what it means to us skaters. They weren't merely our friends; they were constantly in our thoughts. We practiced with them, competed against them, set our standards by their achievements. Why, there wasn't a day, not a day, when Marie and I didn't get together during our practicing, no matter how tight our schedules.

Marie and I . . . Barbara skated faster and faster around the rink, hoping the rush of air would help fight back her tears . . . I can't even think about it. I *won't* think about it.

She became aware of a small group of adults gathered behind the railing. Parents and trainers were talking softly, reading snatches of newspaper stories to one another.

The voice of coach Kate Engstrom rose in anger. "She was always late, always, in the two years that I taught her. Why couldn't she have been late one more time, late enough to have missed that plane!"

Suddenly realizing that Barbara had overheard her, the tall, athletic-looking woman squared her shoulders and said, gruffly, "Come on, everybody. Let's get out on the ice!"

That was Marie that Miss Engstrom was talking about, Barbara knew for sure. Her own friend Marie, the one girl she had confided in, who shared her aims and her ambition.

She couldn't bear to hear any more, couldn't bear to skate, couldn't bear the rink. Her blue eyes overflowing with tears, Barbara made her way quickly toward the elevator. The doors opened just then, and Mrs. McAllister, a newspaper in her hand, the new blue costume over one arm, stood face to face with her daughter, sharing her grief.

All through the following days, everyone Barbara knew talked of nothing but the accident.

The newspapers had written article upon article about all the young skaters involved, the pros, the judges and the parents who had gone along to what was to have been the World Championships. Each item was read and reread, analyzed and commented upon by everyone at the rink. Alongside the feeling of personal grief, there was an overwhelming concern about the future of figure skating in the country. There were hardly any skaters of real caliber left. It was a hard fact to face, but it was true.

Then an article appeared, speculating on the possible makeup of the next United States team. Wide-eyed, Barbara read her own name.

Yes, she knew that she had been considered one of the more promising young competitors. But real prominence had seemed a long, long way off. The United States team? She had yet to compete in the Senior Nationals. And she couldn't do that until she took the Eighth Test! Her coach, for one, wasn't even sure she was ready for that.

Her thoughts rushed ahead. Maybe, if she worked very hard all summer, Vittorio would think her ready for the gold medal test in the fall. But how could she ask him? How could she even talk about it? How could she profit from such a dreadful tragedy? She had always wanted a chance at the top, but never did she think it would present itself in this way!

Torn by conflicting emotions, Barbara put down the newspaper, struggling to sort out her thoughts.

The next day, earlier than usual, Barbara found herself alone at the rink. Her sleep had been filled with a weird succession of images. Skating trophies, burning planes and

9

the smiling face of Marie Whitman had intermingled in her mind all through the night. She had awakened depressed and restless, and decided she might as well get up and spend an extra hour on the ice. Mrs. McAllister, though not overjoyed, had roused herself and fixed their breakfast: coffee and toast for herself, a hamburger and two fried eggs for her daughter.

Now, Barbara limbered up by skating around the rink in a figure eight pattern, going as fast as she could first in one direction and then the other. Through the opaque glass windows she could see the shadows of birds sweeping through the morning air, and she shared some of their sense of freedom and space as she glided over the empty rink.

The ice was still rough from the night before, for she had reached Iceland before the men who would prepare it for the morning session. It took more skill to perform gracefully over the bumps and scratches, but Barbara had seen too many hothouse skaters panic at the sight of an uneven surface. She knew this would be good training for any less manicured rinks she might have to face during competitions abroad.

At the far end of the rink, the Zamboni machine used for resurfacing the ice made its appearance. Barbara waved at the maintenance man, then left the ice to allow him to begin his work. She sat down on a bench and opened her math book, conscious that final exams were only a few weeks off and that she must take advantage of every minute.

Sometimes, especially before exams, she wished that she were more like so many skaters she knew, not really interested in schoolwork. Many were tutored privately, or went to schools for professional children, only to the extent of complying with the education laws. This left them far more time for training, of course. Yet, long ago, while her father was still alive, he had instilled in her a dislike for anything done halfway. Later, the uncompromising private school he had selected had furthered her ambition toward academic distinction. And that, plus her intensive skating program, left very little time for anything else. Including any woolgathering, Barbara reminded herself.

She noticed that a shallow layer of water now lay over the ice and knew that it would soon be frozen hard enough for "patches" to begin. Back to the books, she thought.

She was deep in a math problem when someone sat down next to her. Looking up, she saw her coach lighting his first cigar of the day.

"Barbara," he said between puffs, "I am glad to see you here early."

"I was awake, so I thought I'd get a head start. With finals coming, I'll have to start cutting down on practice time in a few days."

Vittorio nodded, running his hand over his nearly bald head. "I'm glad you are here early because I would like to tell you something."

Barbara closed her book and gave him all her attention.

"I have been offered a position for the summer in Italy, in Cortina, where I grew up." His thoughtful blue eyes studied her reaction carefully. "When I first came to the United States, opportunities for skating teachers were very limited in Italy. But ever since they built a skating stadium in Cortina for the Olympics, I have been anxious to go back there."

Barbara's face clearly showed her disappointment as she searched for something to say.

Vittorio said in a reassuring tone, "It will just be for the summer, you know. Many people go to Cortina to spend their vacation in the Alps, and the stadium is busier then than at any other time of year."

"But I wasn't planning to go anywhere this summer," Barbara interrupted, pique and worry mingled in her voice. "Mother wanted to send me to skating camp, but I told her I wanted to stay right in New York and just train with you." She hesitated. "I wanted to concentrate on my figures for the Eighth Test. That way, perhaps, I could take it in the fall."

"I don't know about that," he broke in, "but you should certainly spend the summer practicing. I would help you find a good pro, you know that."

Barbara had always loved the way he pronounced the word "pro," rolling the "r" and making it sound like an Italian word. Yet, today, she could only think of what he had said and how it would affect her.

Vittorio's voice became very businesslike. "We'll discuss it with your mother when she picks you up for school. Better get on the ice now and go to work."

A few skaters were already out on their "patches," concentrating with complete single-mindedness on their specific figure. Several times a day the ice was divided into sixteen equal sections, each reserved exclusively for one skater who paid for it by the hour. The ice had to be newly scraped and in perfect condition, for it was during these sessions that the skaters traced and retraced the compulsory figures required by the United States Figure Skating Association.

Barbara walked to the entrance closest to her own patch and went right to work on her paragraph loop, a figure which had been giving her some trouble and which was necessary for passing the Eighth Test, the last and most difficult a skater is required to pass.

She executed the figure three times on each foot, as she would be called upon to do during the test. Then, legs slightly apart and straddling the tracings she had made on the ice, she skated all around her paragraph loop, head bent low, carefully studying what she had done.

She straightened up and shook her head, not satisfied with how it looked. The toe of her free foot had touched the ice in several spots. No matter how perfect the rest of her tracing, she would never be forgiven a mistake like that on the day of the test.

Head up, back straight, arms gracefully held, she practiced her figure over and over again. Her mind was not really on it, however. It was filled with concern over the news Vittorio had given her and the effect it might have on her future.

He had been her coach for over five years, ever since she had seriously set her sights on becoming a top-ranking amateur skater. And now that her chances for success seemed better than ever, the thought of beginning with someone new just for the summer made her feel quite lost. And resentful.

Suddenly she stopped.

"That's it!" she burst out loud, and for a moment the scraping and swishing and gliding sounds of the rink came to a stop, while several heads turned to watch her.

Barbara sighed with satisfaction, surprised that such a simple solution hadn't occurred to her right away.

Chapter Three

In the car on the way to school, Barbara started right in on the subject that had been nagging her.

"I saw you talking to Vittorio when I went down to change my clothes," she said quickly to her mother. "I suppose he told you about his summer plans."

Mrs. McAllister gave her a sympathetic glance. "It is a shame, isn't it? Though I can understand his feelings about wanting to get home for a while."

"At first, I didn't know what I'd do," Barbara told her. "But now I think I've got the answer."

Mrs. McAllister seemed surprised. "Well, I'm glad you're not upset anyway. I was afraid you'd balk at having to change teachers over the summer. You never have been a pro-hopper!"

She shifted gears as she turned into the avenue, then continued, "Now that we know we won't have Vittorio in New York, don't you want to consider going to Lake Placid, or some other skating camp?"

"Oh, no, Mother! That wasn't what I meant!"

"It would be much healthier for you than spending the summer in New York. And you could work just as hard."

"But wait, Mother, wait! I've got other plans for us! I want to go to Cortina."

"You *do?*" Mrs. McAllister's voice couldn't have sounded more amazed. "Why, Barbara . . ."

"Oh, please, Mother . . ." Barbara interrupted in the half-imperious, half-appealing tone she used when she most wanted to get her way. "I just can't go through the whole bit of getting used to a new pro for just three months! What difference does it make where I skate, anyway, as long as Vittorio is there?"

"Well, wait a minute! It does make a difference! It's awfully far to go, and it must be terribly expensive."

"It probably doesn't take much longer to fly . . ." Barbara's voice stuck for a second on that word, but she made herself repeat it, "to fly to Italy than to drive to Lake Placid. And you do want me to compete in international championships some day, don't you? So I may as well get used to going abroad!"

Way in the back of her mind, she remembered how she had helped Marie as she packed her bags for her trip to Europe. They had talked excitedly about how some day, perhaps, they both would be on the team. They had joked about their rivalry. . . .

"Barbara, don't change the subject! You can't just ignore the cost!"

"Oh, Mother! You know you've never worried about money when it comes to skating!" Barbara leaped back into the argument, anxious to shake the vision that haunted her.

"Well . . . it's true," Mrs. McAllister nodded, "it is our one major expense. But really . . . going to Cortina! I'm not even sure just where it is! And neither of us knows a word of Italian!"

Barbara leaned over and kissed her mother on the cheek. "Come on, say yes! Vittorio will be there to help us with the language. We don't have to worry about things like that, we'll be at the rink most of the time anyway!"

Mrs. McAllister drove thoughtfully for the next few moments. "Well, it's true that I haven't been to Europe since your father died. And I've never seen the Alps at all. There just might be a nice hotel somewhere near where Vittorio lives. . . ."

"Now get that look out of your eyes!" Barbara interrupted quickly. "This is no sightseeing trip, it's just more hard training!"

"Listen, Barbara, I haven't said 'yes' yet," her mother said forcefully as she drove up to the school entrance. "We'll discuss it with Vittorio after your lesson this afternoon."

But after Barbara had closed the car door behind her and waved good-bye, she called out happily, *"Arrivederci!"*

Vittorio was surprised but delighted at the thought of having his favorite pupil with him over the summer. He shook his head in wonderment and said to Mrs. McAllister, "I should have known our girl Barbara would never take no for an answer!"

"I thought it was a crazy idea, at first," Mrs. McAllister said. "But it does seem a shame to have her change teachers for such a short period. And I guess she'll enjoy the summer. . . ."

Vittorio nodded with vigor. "Oh, I'm sure of that. And you will too, Margaret. Cortina is quite lovely, you know."

"When will we leave, Vittorio?" Barbara wanted to know.

"You will have to wait until the school term is over, Barbara, but I shall have to be there before that."

"Well, then," Mrs. McAllister asked, "will you be able to take care of hotel reservations for us and perhaps rent us a car? It might be less difficult for us to get settled, that way."

"Oh, yes," Vittorio replied, "I'll be glad to lay the groundwork for you! Don't worry, though, Margaret," he reassured her, "you'll have no trouble finding your way about. As a matter of fact," he turned to Barbara, "I have a niece in Cortina who loves to skate too. She's . . . let me see, now . . . about two years older than you, I think. She can be your guide around town."

Barbara nodded casually. "It all sounds just fine to me. I wish we could leave when you do, though."

"No." Vittorio was quite firm. "You need a couple of weeks without skating. It's high time you took a break: I don't want you to get stale. And besides," he reminded her, "you have to wait until your new skates are ready. You certainly can't go abroad with those antiques you're wearing now. The blades are so thin they'll never last the summer!"

Reluctantly, Barbara had to agree.

She didn't enjoy two weeks without skating, however. It was nice sleeping a little later in the mornings, then walking leisurely to school, and she got to see several movies, but quite often she found herself wondering what her school-mates did with all their time.

It might be fun to go to someone's house after school, she was thinking one day as she watched a group of girls walk down the street arm in arm. I guess they must listen to records or look at magazines. Or maybe do their home-work together.

"Happy skating, Barbara!" one of them called out to her, as she started for home.

How do you like that, Barbara thought. They never even noticed I'm not carrying my skates. I guess nobody's used to my having time on my hands. Myself included.

As the end of school approached, however, Barbara really began to feel the excitement of the coming trip. With her mother, she went shopping for airplane luggage. Then they spent a hilarious evening packing and unpacking suitcases and putting them on the bathroom scale to de-termine what clothes would fit into their weight allowance. No matter how they tried, by the time two pairs of skates were weighed in there wasn't much allowance left for anything else. And two pairs of skates it had to be. She had one pair for figures and one pair for free-skating, and they could not be interchanged.

As soon as the decision to go had been made, Mrs. Mc-Allister had called Tozzi's Boot Shop to ask if they could hurry the completion of Barbara's new skates. A few days later, they walked through the door bearing an old-fashioned shoemaker's signpost. Above an oversized high laced boot, NICOLÓ TOZZI was printed in large letters. A woman sitting at the desk looked up from her typewriter and smiled.

"Good morning, Mrs. McAllister. And how are you, Barbara? Excited about your trip? Your boots are ready. Sit down, and my father will be right out to try them on you."

"Mr. Tozzi, himself?" Barbara asked, surprised. "Why, is anything wrong with them?"

"No, no. He just wants to tell you that you're going to the most beautiful country in the world, that's all!" She lowered her voice and continued conspiratorially, "He was all set to fly into one of his rages when he heard you wanted your boots rushed. But when I told him that it was because you were leaving for Italy, he became most understanding!"

Barbara and her mother laughed, remembering a display of temper they had once witnessed when a very young skater had contradicted Mr. Tozzi. Even the most legendary of world champions accepted his advice unquestioningly.

There were some chairs against the wall set aside for fittings, and they sat down to wait. Surrounding Barbara on all sides were hundreds of photographs of skaters, from the smallest tots to ballerinas in glittering costumes, all autographed in most effusive terms. A newspaper clipping of the most recent United States team embarking on what was to be their last trip stunned her as it had when she first saw it in the paper. Images of the friends she had lost swam into her consciousness, crowding out all else.

Then, from behind the partition separating the workshop from the reception area, a tiny, white-haired old man walked in slowly, and she got up to greet him.

"Good morning, Maestro. How wonderful to have you check my skates."

"Oh, my sons, they are all right for fitting most boots," the old man said with a smile, in strongly accented English. "But a pair which is going to Italy must have my blessings first!"

With some difficulty he knelt at Barbara's feet, slipping the soft white leather boots on with loving care, adjusting and admiring them from every angle. One of his sons came in from the adjoining workroom and together they went over every detail of the skates, finally pronouncing them fit for such talented feet.

As they got up to leave, a display case of brightly colored skate bags caught Barbara's eye.

"I could really use a new one of those, Mother," she said, pointing at them through the glass. "My old plaid bag is all worn, inside and out. And I do think these lovely new skates deserve something better. Don't you agree, Mr. Tozzi?"

Chapter Four

On the rack above the passengers' seats, the red skate-shaped bag stood out among the jumble of blankets and jackets. The impeccable young stewardess noticed it immediately as she came down the aisle of the plane just before takeoff.

"I'm sorry, miss, you'll have to take down that"—she hesitated over her choice of words—"pocket book? No bags are permitted on the shelf."

Barbara got up to comply with her request and placed the bag on the floor between her mother and herself. As she leaned back in her seat, a dark, pig-tailed head peeked around her shoulder.

"Is that a Christmas stocking? In July?" The child's voice was incredulous.

"No." Barbara laughed. "It's a skate bag. It does look like a Christmas stocking, doesn't it?"

She had found her first pair of skates in a similar bag, under the Christmas tree, years ago. She had thought it would be filled with toys and candy, Barbara suddenly remembered, and had been terribly disappointed when she found out it wasn't!

The roar of the engine getting ready for takeoff cut

short their conversation, and the little girl sat back behind Barbara.

The plane rose and the light went off under the FASTEN YOUR SEAT BELT sign. Barbara removed hers, burrowing back into the seat. She recalled her first skating lesson, that winter after she had had such a bad case of measles. Her father, himself a doctor, had suggested to the pediatrician that some form of outdoor exercise might help her regain her strength. The pediatrician had turned to her then, asking what sport she liked best, and Barbara had mentioned that she had a pair of skates which she had hardly ever used.

"We'll see if they still fit, and we'll sign you up for some skating lessons," she could remember her father saying.

Before long she was learning cross-overs and skating backward, and when spring came and the rink in Central Park closed for the season, she had begged her parents to let her continue throughout the summer at an indoor arena.

At Iceland she had met children and young people who were vitally interested in the sport. Some were even considered champion material, although they were younger than she. This single-minded, self-sufficient world had fascinated Barbara from the very first. Soon she was explaining to her parents the system of tests set up by the United States Figure Skating Association, and the school figures she would be required to learn if they agreed to let her try.

For her tenth birthday, Dr. and Mrs. McAllister had given Barbara a membership to the local Figure Skating Club, and that winter she had taken her preliminary test.

She had passed quite easily: practicing her skating edges and her waltz eight over and over until the tracings were satisfactory had been a challenging experience for her.

Then came the surprising moment when she heard her teacher say to her father, as he stood with his arm proudly around Barbara's shoulder, "I think your daughter has outgrown me, Dr. McAllister. I only teach the very beginners, and I think Barbara has the makings of a some-day champion, if she continues to be as conscientious as she is now. She has the grace and precision which are essential." Then he had offered a suggestion. "There is a new pro recently arrived from Europe; he was an Olympic skater, and I understand he works very well with young people. You'd be fortunate if he agreed to take on Barbara."

From then on Vittorio Bianchi had become Barbara's coach, watching over each step of her development as a skater yet working closely with her father to see that her schooling didn't suffer.

After Dr. McAllister's death, his wife had dedicated herself exclusively to helping Barbara. She didn't seem to want any activities or social contacts of her own; her days were filled to capacity as it was.

"Look, Barbie, we're flying over the ocean now. We really are on our way!"

Mrs. McAllister's voice broke into Barbara's reminiscences. Drowsily, she leaned across her mother to look out of the window. I must have been almost asleep, she thought as she stared at the enormous expanse of ocean. Night was coming on, and the water was a dark blue, broken up here and there by tiny white dots. Seagulls, she wondered? Then she smiled as she realized that they were actually mountainous waves, made insignificant by the great height of the plane.

She sat back in her seat again. Here I am, on my way to

Europe, she marveled, and how much has happened since that preliminary test!

From that point on, tests and competitions had followed one another in rapid succession. Subsectional tournaments, then the Easterns, the Junior Nationals, with the Nationals and the World Championships yet to go. And, of course, some day the Olympics.

Meanwhile, the jewelry box in her suitcase held her bronze and silver medals: bronze for the first three tests, silver for passing four through seven. The Eighth Test, and that much desired gold medal, was now the immediate goal.

Not that all the medals had been easily won, not by a long shot. Barbara would always remember that first time she had failed a test. She had walked off the ice with several other youngsters, and the judges had gone into a huddle in the small office next door. Then they had called her in and told her, as kindly as they could, what her mistakes had been.

Unable to hold back her tears, she had run off to the dressing room. Neither her mother's comforting words nor Vittorio's assurances that she could take the test again in two months had eased her disappointment. It had been an older girl, there to take a more advanced test, who had talked of her own setbacks and convinced Barbara that failure could actually sharpen her ability.

And this, Barbara recalled sadly, had been the start of her friendship with Marie Whitman. Barbara had found herself moving further and further away from the girls at school, but it didn't seem to make any difference. The interests that bound her to Marie were what really mattered to both of them. She wondered how long it would be before she would again find such complete kinship with another person.

Barbara could feel her eyes closing, and she let herself be lulled by the quiet hum of the motor as the plane brought her closer to her Italian summer. When she awoke, it was to hear the pilot's voice coming over the loudspeaker.

"Ladies and gentlemen, we are now approaching Mont Blanc. We will circle the mountain so you may see it from both sides of the plane."

Barbara rubbed her eyes, saw her mother smiling at her.

"You certainly did get a good night's sleep, dear. You're just in time for breakfast."

The plane tilted slightly toward their side as it banked around a curve. Just like a perfectly skated cross-over, Barbara smiled to herself. Framed in the window she now saw a sky of brightest blue and mountains crowned with shimmering white snow.

"Oh, Mother, look! Do you think Cortina will be anything like that?"

Nose to the glass and looking straight below, Barbara could see where the snow ended and the dark green of the pine forest began. This, in turn, gave way to the softer green of a tranquil valley. Cutting through this tapestry was a silver thread of water, edged on both sides by a scatter of rooftops.

Mrs. McAllister thought for a moment.

"Well, no, I don't think so, from what Vittorio told us. Cortina must be a larger village than that."

For a while they tried to guess what kind of surroundings lay in wait for them. Soon the stewardess stopped by with their breakfast coffee and pastries and told them that within half an hour they would be landing in Milan.

She had been dreading that moment, Barbara suddenly realized. It was just before the landing that the plane carrying the skating team had crashed and burned. All through the trip she had pushed this fear to the back of her mind, but now it was uppermost. She could hardly wait to set foot safely on airport concrete.

Reluctant to tell her mother of her fears, she sat with her eyes closed, fighting a twinge of airsickness.

"You look a little pale, Barbie. Shall I get you some gum from the stewardess?"

"Okay. Yes, please," she answered unhappily.

The gum helped, and soon the plane's jolting told her they were touching the runway. Barbara sighed with relief as the door swung open.

Understandingly, Mrs. McAllister put her arm around her daughter's shoulders and gave her a brief hug, then preceded her down into the hot, dusty Milan day.

Chapter Five

*T*he phone rang in their hotel room early next morning, and the desk clerk announced to Mrs. McAllister that their car was waiting outside.

With a happy whoop, Barbara sat on the lid of her suitcase to close it more quickly, and they hurried downstairs. Both were eager to see what kind of car Vittorio had arranged for them to rent during their stay in Italy. It turned out to be a small, cream-colored Giulietta, and the man who had driven it over explained its workings in great detail and told them, in painstaking English, that it had great power on mountain roads.

At this, Mrs. McAllister looked somewhat intimidated and ventured to suggest that perhaps they should spend the day driving around the outskirts of Milan, while she got accustomed to Italian roads.

"Oh, Mother, no!" Barbara broke in. "We saw enough of Milan yesterday afternoon, and I can't wait to get to Cortina and start working!"

"Barbara, how can you say 'enough of Milan'? All we saw was the cathedral!"

She didn't argue with Barbara, though, and instead motioned to the bellboy to start loading the car.

Soon they were driving along a broad, smooth highway, noticing fertile fields geometrically divided by rows of poplars, and grape vines strung between mulberry trees. As they sped on they became aware of a gray, cloudlike shadow all along the horizon.

"Look, Barbie," Mrs. McAllister pointed ahead, "I think that must be the Alps."

"Oh, good," Barbara replied lightly. "Then it won't be long."

Yet, it was considerably longer than they had expected, for as soon as they reached the foothills, the road began to narrow down and twist through colorful small towns.

True to its reputation, their little car took admirably to the frequent ascents. For all her experience behind the wheel, Mrs. McAllister found herself gasping at the nonchalance with which native drivers maneuvered past her on the roller coaster road.

Suddenly, a group of children on the side of the road seemed to be flagging them down, and Mrs. McAllister slowed to a stop. Barbara rolled down her window, leaned out and saw that they were waving tight little bouquets of soft purple flowers. Quick to recognize a foreign tourist, the children pushed their flowers close to her nose, all the while chattering in rapid Italian. Mrs. McAllister reached past her daughter for one of the posies, inhaled the pungent fragrance and exclaimed, "Why, look, they must be cyclamens! But how tiny! I wonder if they grow wild around here!"

"Let's buy some, otherwise they'll never move away from our car," Barbara urged.

Her mother handed the children some money, over

which they were loudly squabbling as the car drove on.

Shortly thereafter the scenery began to change again, and Barbara caught her breath at the sight of the snow-capped Dolomite mountains rising behind each turn in the road. They drove through several small resort towns, post-card bright, with flowers growing in tiny gardens and hundreds of window boxes on the wooden chalets.

Then suddenly there was Cortina, stretched across a whole valley and overflowing up the side of the mountains, a seemingly endless circle of rocky peaks enclosing it on all sides.

They followed the hotel manager down the hall toward their room, and the first thing Barbara wanted to know was the location of the skating rink.

He unlocked the door and promptly went to the window, pointing proudly to the rooftops below.

"It is at the other end of the town, farther down in the valley, but you can see it from here. Look, do you see that green . . . hmm, how do you say it in English . . . canopy? That is the roof of the stadium."

Barbara turned from the view. "Can we go right down, Mother? Please? Come on, let's unpack later!"

Mrs. McAllister winced. "Oh, Barbie! I've been driving for hours!"

The manager, his hand on the doorknob, cleared his throat in polite interruption.

"Mr. Bianchi stopped by this morning. Those flowers are from him," he said, nodding toward a nearby table. "He asked that you call him when you arrive. He'll be at the rink."

"Let's go and surprise him, Mother. Don't you want to?" Barbara asked pleadingly.

The manager turned to Mrs. McAllister.

"I shall go now, but please call me if you need anything." Then he added, "The hotel has a bus which goes into town every hour. It will go as far as the skating rink, if you ask the driver." He smiled at Barbara, "*Pattinaggio* is Italian for skating rink."

After the door was closed, Mrs. McAllister turned to Barbara. "You could go on the bus, I guess, if you wanted to go right now."

"How could I?" Barbara looked aghast. "I don't know my way around the town, and I can't speak Italian. And besides . . ." she brightened considerably, "don't you want to see the stadium too? We can wait a little while, if you like!"

Mrs. McAllister walked toward the bed, patted the soft eiderdown which lay folded in a triangle, then sat down wearily.

"Okay Barbara, I'll lie down for ten minutes, and then drive you into town. Ten minutes, that's all."

A half hour later they parked at the entrance to the large arena. Inside, a green canvas awning protected the ice from sun and rain, casting an odd light over the few skaters at work. Barbara immediately spotted Vittorio on the ice with a tall, blond girl. His voice was stern, and in spitfire Italian he was explaining a movement to his pupil. In reply to a command, she placed her hand on his back so she could feel the way his muscles moved, as Barbara herself had done so many times.

31

When he straightened up he saw the McAllisters and in one graceful streak across the ice was at their side, both hands outstretched. He wanted to hear all about their trip, and they told him how pleased they were with their car and the hotel accommodations.

"Can I start skating today?" Barbara asked, pleased with the size of the rink and the apparent lack of overcrowding.

"Tomorrow, Barbara," Vittorio replied. "I have already made arrangements for you to start patches at 6:30. Is that early enough for you?"

There was a teasing look in his eyes as he spoke. Suddenly, he raised his eyebrows and clapped his hand to his head. Turning around, he waved to the pupil he had left standing on the ice, beckoning her to his side.

"Mrs. McAllister, this is my niece, Fiammetta Bianchi. And this is Barbara, who I hope will be your friend."

The two girls smiled at each other.

"I had pictured you quite differently. . . ." Barbara began.

"We mountain people don't look much like Italians are supposed to look," Fiammetta replied in charmingly accented English. "You, however, are exactly as Zio Vittorio described you. And I am most anxious to see you skate, Barbara."

When Fiammetta said the name, the *a*'s were broad, the *r*'s were rolled, and the whole effect was so new and musical that Barbara turned to her mother and said, "For the first time in my life, I really like my own name!"

Chapter Six

*T*he next morning, after two hours of intensive patches, Barbara walked off the ice delighted with the world at large. She had found it exhilarating to skate in the mountain air. The surrounding peaks were in full view, and the snow fields gleamed brighter than ever in the early sun.

In the downstairs dressing room, Fiammetta sat down next to her to remove her skates.

"How was your first night in Cortina? Did you sleep well?" Fiammetta wanted to know. "Did you find the skating more tiring in this high altitude?"

Barbara shook her head. "Not so far, though I may notice it more by this evening. But I certainly am hungry! There was no one in the dining room when we left the hotel. Doesn't anyone get up early around here?"

A smile brightened Fiammetta's face. "Not at the large hotels! There *are* people who start out very early in Cortina, the ones who come for mountain climbing, but they don't usually stay at such elegant places."

Barbara looked surprised. "Oh, do people come here to climb mountains? Do you do that?" she asked, as she pulled on her white turtleneck sweater.

"Sometimes, on Sunday, or when I'm not working. I

33

don't get many chances nowadays, though. I used to go along with my father during school vacations. He is a guide, you know; he takes groups of people on excursions, and I frequently acted as interpreter for him, if the visitors were from abroad."

While she explained, Fiammetta had briefly disappeared into one of the dressing rooms, and she emerged clad in a gay blue dirndl dress, printed all over with hearts, flowers and dancing couples. She tied the bow on a contrasting apron and looked up to see Barbara eyeing her admiringly.

"How pretty you look. Is that what the girls wear here?"

Fiammetta looked a little self-conscious. "Well, it's what all the women *used* to wear in the old days. These days, most girls only wear the local costume on holidays, or to church on Sundays. But *I* have to wear it every day, because my boss at the toy shop likes his sales girls dressed this way."

As they walked up the steps from the dressing room together, Barbara spotted her mother sitting at the coffee shop, which was at the edge of the rink.

"Will you have some breakfast with us?" Barbara asked. "I hadn't realized you worked. Do you have to go right now?"

Fiammetta nodded. "Yes, I'm afraid I do. The store opens at ten."

"But I thought you were a skater. How do you manage to fit that in? And don't you go to school?"

"No, I don't go to school any more. I finished last June." Fiammetta stole a glance at her watch. "Before I graduated,

34

I used to work at the toy shop only in the summer, but now I do it full time. I have always hoped that some day I could get a job skating, but until then I can only do it in my free moments. Now," she added, "I really have to go. Would you like to meet me on Sunday? I'm free then, and we can talk some more. I'd love to show you around the town."

U. S. 1347594

"I'd like that very much," said Barbara, as she waved good-bye and walked over to join her mother.

It was her first attempt at ordering a meal in Italian, and Barbara did not find it easy. The waiter spoke no English, and though she looked up the word for "steak" in her pocket dictionary, all he did was spread out his arms and shake his head.

During the fruitless exchange, Barbara and Mrs. McAllister suddenly saw a tall, dark young man walking over to their table, an amused smile on his face.

"It is not the custom in Italy to have such hearty breakfasts," he explained in a deep voice. "But perhaps I could help you order something that would satisfy your appetite?" He made a slight bow in the direction of Mrs. McAllister. "May I introduce myself? My name is Dario Visconti. I believe I saw you at the hotel last evening."

His tone was most courteous, and only his dark eyes showed amusement. Mrs. McAllister, charmed by his manner, hurried to explain that her daughter had had no breakfast and had been skating for hours.

After due deliberation, Barbara decided on two fried eggs and a cheese sandwich, which turned out to be a thick roll with a delicious hunk of local cheese.

35

"You have already skated today, Signorina?" Dario turned to Barbara. "But the rink does not open until ten-thirty. I came a little early to try to avoid the crowds."

"That must be the public session," Barbara explained in a matter-of-fact tone. "I can't skate when there are so many people."

"Oh, are you a professional?"

"Heavens, no! I'm an amateur skater." She drank the last drop of her hot chocolate and said to no one in particular, "I wish people drank milk around here! I wonder if they have any at the hotel?"

She thought she heard the young man chuckle, but when she looked up, his face was serious and attentive. She turned to her mother, feeling annoyed and slightly unsure.

"Could we go back now for a while, Mother? I'm really bushed. Maybe the altitude is bothering me after all."

Then they rose to leave and thanked Dario. Aghast, Barbara saw him bend low and kiss her hand. She barely heard him say that he looked forward to seeing them again, at the hotel.

Sunday morning Barbara made her way toward the church where she had arranged to meet Fiammetta. The town was jammed with chic visitors promenading through the cobblestoned streets, and today they were joined by the townspeople, many of whom wore dirndl dresses similar to Fiammetta's.

It was the custom in Cortina to close off the center of the village to all vehicles during the hour before lunch and dinner, when the visitors most enjoyed strolling and window-shopping. Barbara soon surrendered the crowded sidewalk and moved onto the middle of the street, and a few moments later she caught sight of Fiammetta.

"We have a beautiful day, Barbara. What would you most like to do?" The Italian girl smiled in greeting.

"Well, you mentioned the mountains the other day. Could we see something of them?"

Fiammetta looked at her own neat cotton suit, then at Barbara's bright summer dress.

"We're not really dressed for hiking. I'll tell you what might be fun, though. We could take the *funivia* up Mt. Faloria."

Barbara looked thoroughly puzzled, and Fiammetta pointed upward.

"That's Mt. Faloria, straight ahead of us. There is a *funivia*, a little car that hangs from a cable, which goes all the way up to the top, and one gets a beautiful view from there without having to walk too much."

"That sounds like a good idea," Barbara agreed. "To tell you the truth, I've been having some trouble with the heel of my right foot—has that ever happened to you? Please don't mention it in front of my mother, though, or she'll keep me off the ice."

"It's happened to me with new skates," Fiammetta nodded. "Yours must be new; I have admired them. Skates are so expensive here," she added, "that I have not had a new pair since my feet stopped growing."

As they talked, Fiammetta steered her friend away from the church square, past several cafes where people sat at outdoor tables. On the steps of one small restaurant, an overflow group of elegant visitors sat holding their glasses of vermouth. Barbara must have looked surprised, because

37

Fiammetta laughed and said, "Oh, those are not just ordinary steps! That's the most fashionable spot in Cortina for seeing and being seen. It's almost as chic as the wearing of suede jackets and coats this summer. Have you noticed how many there are? It's the uniform of the Milanese and the Venetians when they come for their change of air."

No, Barbara thought, surprised at the edge in Fiammetta's voice, she had not noticed. In fact, it occurred to her that she had noticed remarkably little of her new surroundings, what with skating three times a day. She had just barely found time for buying a wool skirt and two thick sweaters to ward off the unexpectedly cool weather.

Fiammetta was silent as they went through several back streets toward the railroad station. A blue electrified train had just pulled in, and it looked like a small boy's dream of the ideal toy.

"We're not taking that, are we?" Barbara asked.

"No, our *funivia* is in that shed over there. See that line of people waiting to get on?" And as they headed toward it, Fiammetta added, "I didn't mean to sound nasty before, when I spoke about the wealthy visitors, but sometimes it gets difficult to . . . to . . ."

"To have to work so hard?" Barbara tried to finish the sentence for her.

"No, I don't mind the work, although I do prefer skating. It's just that the town changes so in the tourist seasons. The crowds and the noise and the way they just take over."

Inside the shed, they bought their tickets, then stepped into the oval-shaped car, waiting for it to start.

Frowning, Barbara thought more about her friend's last statement.

"But why should the tourists' coming bother you? You have your own life here."

Fiammetta smiled wryly. "It's because everyone in the town depends on them so much, I suppose. We work for them in hotels or stores, we drive their cars, or guide them through the mountains; we teach them to ski or skate. We couldn't exist without them—that's why we resent them, I guess."

Barbara looked uncomfortable, and Fiammetta quickly laid a hand on her arm.

"I didn't mean you, and please excuse me for carrying on this way. I was sure we'd be friends from the moment Zio Vittorio told me about you. In fact, you're the first outsider with whom I've ever had a serious talk."

I haven't confided in anyone for quite a while, either, Barbara thought, feeling, for a moment, quite disloyal to the friend she had lost. Yet she found herself very drawn to this girl who so freely offered her help and friendship.

After a few more people had entered the cable car, the doors closed and they began to move. Once out of the shed, the *funivia* rode smoothly above the meadows surrounding the town. Through the glass enclosure Barbara could see children playing in the sun, while their parents relaxed nearby, enjoying their Sunday leisure.

Up ahead, the wires that held the cable car stretched in an upward curve toward the mountain, and soon the dark green of the pine forest was below them. In occasional clearings between trees they could see small mountain lakes and tiny dots of moving color.

"I must take you for a hike through those woods." Fiammetta's voice made Barbara turn away from the window near which she stood, peering down at the distant landscape. "They are almost like an enchanted forest."

The two girls stood with their heads close together, noses pressed against the glass.

"Look down there," Fiammetta continued, "by that little pond. That must be people picking wild flowers, or perhaps strawberries."

"Can one skate on those lakes in the winter?"

"The lakes do freeze, but they are always covered with snow, and most people don't bother to clear them. Nobody much ever skated around here until they built the Olympic Stadium. And I'm not sure I ever would have, if my uncle were not a pro," Fiammetta went on. "My parents don't really approve. It's too expensive."

A slight jarring of the cable car made Barbara look out of the window, and she realized that they had begun the steepest part of the ascent. To her astonishment, the *funivia* appeared to be rising parallel to the rock. Below them was a seemingly bottomless abyss.

Startled, she drew back from the window. Next to her, a woman leaned against the wall of the cabin with her eyes closed, drops of perspiration forming on her forehead.

It was Fiammetta who turned to the lady and spoke softly to her in Italian. To Barbara's unspoken question, she replied:

"I told her we were almost at the top, and that she could get care, if she needed it, when we got to the *rifugio*."

A few moments later Barbara tried again to look out of the window, fascinated by the void below.

"Does it bother you too?" Fiammetta asked solicitously. "Don't look outside, if it does."

Barbara managed to break the spell that the hypnotic view seemed to hold for her.

"What was that word you used before, when you said that lady could get help when we got off?" she asked, only half in jest.

Fiammetta laughed. "*Rifugio?* That means refuge. It's a little chalet, a hostel where you can get food or first aid, or overnight accommodations, if you want them. You'll find many of them in the Alps, on almost all the mountains. But you won't need any help, or smelling salts, believe me. You'll be fine as soon as we're on the ground."

The cable car was coming to a stop, and the two girls stepped out with the other passengers.

The contrast with the landscape below was so startling that Barbara stopped and looked around in amazement. No trees were in sight and very little greenery. Rocks and boulders and a few scrubby bushes covered the plateau on which they stood.

"Let's walk over to the *rifugio*. From there you can really see for miles around."

Fiammetta took Barbara's hand, and they walked the few hundred feet until they came to a brown chalet. On the terrace, people were sunning themselves in deck chairs. The two girls walked over to the edge of the plateau to get the best possible view.

Now, on a level with her eyes, Barbara recognized many of the same strangely shaped mountains she had seen from Cortina below. Some reached toward the skyline like finely etched stalagmites; others resembled abstract sculptures.

Way in the distance, one was topped by what seemed to be
five medieval towers, side by side. Everywhere she looked,
new peaks emerged, some far higher than where she stood,
others partly hidden by clouds.

She turned to Fiammetta. "It all makes one feel very
small, doesn't it? Almost unimportant. And that doesn't
often happen to me!" she laughed at herself.

A loud guffaw resounded behind them, and a decidedly
English, decidedly male voice exclaimed sarcastically,

"Oh, I say! 'Almost unimportant?' "

Chapter Seven

The two girls turned quickly around to see who had spoken. A fair young man of medium height, wearing shorts, woolen knee socks and heavy climbing boots was smiling at them.

"I was almost asleep in one of those chairs over there," he explained apologetically. "I walked over when I heard the King's English. Though it's not really the King's, is it? Are you girls both American?"

Fiammetta laughed. "Oh, no! I am Italian, but my friend is from New York."

He extended a sunburned, calloused hand. "I'm Neil Adamson, from Cambridge. I'm sorry if I seemed rude before," he said, turning to Barbara. "It's just that I'm so constantly overwhelmed by these mountains, your remark jarred a bit. May I offer you a cup of hot chocolate to make up for my intrusion?"

Barbara looked at Fiammetta questioningly.

"Oh, let's!" Fiammetta nodded. "They have wonderful whipped cream at the *rifugio*."

Neil and Barbara both laughed, and the three of them walked into the dark, paneled taproom of the chalet. Neil led them to a corner table and ordered their refreshments.

43

As the proprietress turned toward the kitchen, Neil called her back.

"*C'è torta di cioccolata oggi, Signora?*"

Fiammetta looked at him in surprise. "How did you know about their special chocolate cake? And where did you learn your Italian?"

Neil finished the ordering, then replied lightly,

"If you have a week or two to listen, I'd be glad to tell you the story of my life!"

"Well, never mind the early childhood," Barbara interrupted, amused by his manner. "Just tell us how you learned Italian! I wish I could!"

She was surprised to hear herself say that, and even more surprised to realize that she honestly did wish she knew a little of that lilting, musical tongue which she heard all about her.

"I've been coming here for a number of years," Neil explained. "You see, I love to hike, especially in these mountains. I fell in love with the Dolomites when I came on holiday with my family, and I've been back each summer since then."

He stopped to thank the proprietress as she laid before them the fragrant cups of hot chocolate and the much heralded cake, and Barbara asked, "Do you stay here, at the *rifugio?*" She hesitated before the Italian word, feeling self-conscious. "Or are you at a hotel in Cortina?"

"Oh, no," Neil replied, taking a well-worn pipe out of his pocket and filling it with tobacco. "Cortina is too expensive for a poor university student. I hike from one *rifugio* to another, sometimes with friends, sometimes

44

alone, and I occasionally stop at some of the less rustic spots to get a taste of civilization, like today."

"What do you study at college," Barbara wanted to know, "languages?"

Neil shook his head. "Italian is my favorite avocation, but actually I'm in architecture."

Fiammetta interrupted amicably. "Here we are, asking you a thousand questions, and we haven't even told you our names! My friend is Barbara McAllister, and I am Fiammetta Bianchi. Tell us, Mr. Adamson, how far are you going today, or will you be stopping here overnight?"

"I haven't any plans for the rest of the day, Fiammetta, and please call me Neil! Would you both like to join me in a hike to the top of the mountain?"

Barbara turned to her friend.

"What do you think, Fiammetta? I'd like to go up farther, but I'm not sure that I should with my heel the way it is."

"Oh, we'll do it some other time," Fiammetta replied without hesitation. "You've got to rest that foot or you might miss some of your skating sessions next week. And Zio Vittorio would never forgive me."

Neil had risen to pay the cashier when he caught the last sentence. "Say no more until I've paid the bill," he said over his shoulder. "I've told you all about myself, but now I'm anxious to hear about you two."

The two girls walked out into the sunlight, and Neil followed a few seconds later.

"What's all this about skating? And whose Uncle Victor is such an ogre?"

The girls took turns at telling him about themselves. Sitting in the old-fashioned canvas deck chairs on the terrace, they described their separate loves for skating and how Vittorio Bianchi had influenced both their lives.

"And just this morning Zio Vittorio told me," Fiammetta was summing up her part of the story, "that an American ice show, which has been touring Europe, is going to perform at the stadium in Cortina. He knows the man in charge and is going to write him to ask if I might audition for them."

Barbara leaned toward Fiammetta excitedly. "Oh, how marvelous! Then you might come to the States with the show! Why didn't you tell me before?"

Fiammetta's gaze wandered over the distant peaks. "Oh, well, none of it might come true at all. I haven't even dared discuss it with my parents. And very likely they won't let me join a professional company even if I should do well in the audition."

Neil turned to Barbara. "How about you? Will you be trying out also?"

Barbara shook her head with determination. "No, no. If you earn money as a skater, you lose your amateur status and can no longer compete."

Neil gave her a long, quizzical look. "And is competition an end in itself for you?" He laughed. "Your aim then is to be the world champion?"

"Yes," replied Barbara softly. "Some day, if I can."

Neil looked toward Fiammetta for confirmation, dumbfounded. Quickly, the Italian girl interjected, "It's not all that farfetched, you know. You should see her skate! Some day you'll be proud to say you knew her!"

Neil was clearly fascinated by both of them. "And you, Fiammetta, do you have this competitive spirit too?"

"I might have had it once, when I first discovered skating," she replied, a thoughtful expression crossing her face. "I do think one is more likely to become a really fine athlete if one has an immediate goal . . . a test, or a competition. But my family could never afford the life of an amateur skater. I'd be quite satisfied, though, if I could earn my living that way."

Barbara pensively rubbed the heel that bothered her. "I suppose I should consider getting back to the hotel and bathing this foot of mine. I have a big day coming up tomorrow. Strange . . ." she continued, "how people's noses wrinkle up at the very mention of the word 'competitiveness.'"

Neil promptly wrinkled his nose at her, and Barbara went on, defensively, "In skating, at any rate, it's not a question of one man pinning the other to the ground, it's more the idea of achieving . . . or striving to achieve . . . perfection of movement, for its own sake. Not for the sake of beating any one else. Is that such a bad thing to aim for?"

"No, Barbara, I didn't mean to imply that it was. In fact, it's quite admirable for a young slip of a girl to have such definite ambitions. Only . . . I don't know . . . it's a world I know nothing about, I suppose. Could I come and watch you tomorrow, do you think, while you're out on the ice achieving perfection?"

As Barbara made her way from the dressing room to the rink the next morning, she looked around to see if Neil really had come to see her skate, as he had said he would. The benches around the ice were almost empty at that early hour, however, and no shaggy blond head was in evidence. She welcomed the chance to warm up without his quizzical glance upon her, although, she realized as she slid toward the center of the rink, she did hope he would make an appearance. She had really enjoyed talking to him, even enjoyed his teasing, she thought in surprise. At home, she had been shy with boys, but everything seemed different for her here.

Within a short time she had lost all consciousness of any audience. Even the soreness of her heel, which had bothered her as she put on the skates, was pushed out of awareness as she concentrated all her efforts on the paragraph double three. Why this figure had been so difficult for her to master was something of a mystery both to Barbara and to her coach.

This morning, she set herself to it as if it were the first time, repeating to herself the basic rules about dividing the circle into three equal curves. The middle curve should be skated so that it is divided into halves by the long axis of the figure. Barbara repeated the rule to herself as she worked it out on the ice. She had always enjoyed the mathematical neatness of the set patterns for school figures. She got as much satisfaction out of solving these as she did from the more complex formulae in her science courses at school.

Slowly, carefully, her tongue following the outline of her lip in rapt concentration, Barbara skated the figure through. Right forward outside, three times; then left forward inside, three times; then left forward outside and right forward inside, three times each for all the changes of blade edge and direction, her mind making a singsong of the words. As she completed the right backward inside paragraph bracket, she heard a soft hand clapping. Vittorio was leaning on the wooden railing, a pleased smile on his lean face.

"That's it, Barbara! You're finally getting it!"

She turned and skated swiftly toward him, delighted at his reaction.

"Do you really think so? It felt right, but I wasn't sure how it looked."

"Well, you can certainly use more practice. Your flow wasn't even enough, and you were much too busy watching your feet, but technically it was fine, and the rest will come as you relax."

Suddenly, stepping carefully on the ice in his climbing boots, Neil Adamson appeared behind Vittorio, and Barbara realized that she had been so intent on her practicing that she had neglected to watch for his arrival.

"I gather you've had a successful morning. Congratulations! I must say I rather expected you to be leaping and whirling and all that sort of thing rather than this sober performance!"

Barbara laughed. "You'll have to come back during free skating time if you want to be dazzled! What you just saw was the more scientific end of things!"

She turned to Vittorio. "This is Neil Adamson, whom we met at the *rifugio* yesterday, Fiammetta and I. And here comes my mother, all ready to drive me back to the hotel. Mother, this is Neil Adamson."

"How do you do, Mrs. McAllister, Mr. Bianchi."

Vittorio turned to Mrs. McAllister and said in a business-like tone, "Margaret, could you and Barbara stay a while? I'd like very much to speak with you."

Neil seemed disappointed. "I had hoped that you could spend some time with me now that you're through skating. Would it be all right if I came back for you in an hour?"

"I don't think you'd better, Neil," Mrs. McAllister replied for Barbara. "I want her to come back to the hotel with me and soak her heel before she skates again. In fact, she probably shouldn't be skating at all, it looks so sore."

Barbara threw her mother a mortified look.

Unaware of the rising tension, Vittorio put his hand on Barbara's elbow, anxious to get started on their conference.

"Shall we talk over coffee? I don't have much time before the public session begins, and my other students claim me."

Barbara shrugged uncomfortably. "Today looks pretty hopeless, Neil. I'm sorry. But I'm awfully glad you came down this morning."

"I won't be around for the next couple of days," Neil said. "I'm due to join some English friends a little way from here. I should be back by the weekend, though. Would you and Fiammetta like to do some sight-seeing with me on Sunday? I assume she doesn't work then and that you take the day off too?"

Barbara accepted eagerly and followed her mother and Vittorio, who were already walking toward the coffee shop.

50

Neil called after her, "I'll call you Saturday morning!" and turned to leave.

Glowering, Barbara slipped into the chair next to her mother's.

"You really didn't have to describe my foot in all its gory details, did you, Mother? Neil will think I'm an infant! How could you have embarrassed me so in front of a stranger?"

"But Barbara . . ." Mrs. McAllister started to explain. Vittorio didn't give her a chance to continue.

"Please, Margaret. Barbara. Save your arguments for later. What's come over you this morning, anyway, Barbara? I must talk to you seriously. Please listen to me."

Belatedly aware of the urgency in his tone, Barbara turned her attention to him.

"I'm sorry, Vittorio. What was it you wanted to tell me?"

"Something you've no doubt been waiting to hear for weeks. Simply that I think you've made very good progress since you've been in Cortina, and that I want you to take your gold medal test just as soon as you get back to New York. And, at the same time, I want us to start thinking of a free-skating routine good enough for the Nationals."

Barbara leaned excitedly toward Vittorio. "The Nationals? Do you think I'm ready? Is that why you want me to take the Eighth Test as soon as I get to New York? Who will I be competing against?"

She stopped and looked questioningly at her teacher.

Vittorio knew what was on her mind. "I don't know,

Barbara. There aren't very many girls ready for the Nationals this year."

Mrs. McAllister moved her hand forward as if to stop his words, but he went on.

"I know you don't like to talk about the crash, Barbara. But you do know what a void it has left in American skating. From letters I have received . . . and you know, skating pros are not the best correspondents . . . I know that there are some young people working out this summer, but I can't imagine their being any better than you. You and they are the top, now."

A million thoughts had been whirling through Barbara's head as he spoke. What she had tried to push into the back of her mind ever since the plane crashed had now come out into the open. It was exciting to be considered ready for the Nationals. True, it was what she had been waiting to hear. Yet, now that the words had been said out loud, she didn't know if she could bear to be replacing her friends. The very thought sickened her.

Tears came into her eyes as she searched for words to express her feelings. "I would feel so . . . disloyal, skating in the Nationals, Vittorio. It would be as if . . . as if I were taking someone else's place."

"But you have to take their place, Barbara. Someone has to rebuild the team. And you are a fine skater. You owe it to yourself, as well as to skating, to take this opportunity."

"I was sure you'd feel this way, dear," Mrs. McAllister said softly. "But look, Barbie, your time would have come anyway. Later, to be sure, if the crash hadn't robbed us of the others, but even they would not have been champions forever. And you have been working toward it for a long time."

Barbara nodded. "I know, I know. It's just that the way is being paved for me by such horrible events."

"The way is not being paved for you," Vittorio interrupted forcefully. "It's been shortened somewhat, that's all. Don't start believing that it's going to be so easy: there may be some fine talent shaping up this summer. All I'm saying is that you should aim for the Nationals, regardless of who else may enter them."

A polite cough interrupted the intense conversation. The same attractive young man who had helped Barbara order her first Italian breakfast suddenly materialized at Vittorio's side.

"Ah, Signor Visconti. I'm sorry I kept you waiting," Vittorio said to him in Italian. "I lost track of the time."

"Not at all." Dario's reply was in English. "I only interrupt because it gives me the opportunity to greet Mrs. McAllister and her charming daughter. I had no idea we shared the same teacher!"

Vittorio pushed his chair back, telling Dario that he would join him on the ice in a second. As he watched Dario bow and walk away, Vittorio muttered, half to himself, "He'll think himself as good a skater as you are, now that he knows I'm your coach. I have no idea why he takes lessons at all, anyway. He's convinced he can do everything to perfection."

Still talking, he followed his pupil in the direction of the rink.

Relieved that the tense conversation was at an end, Bar-

bara smiled at her mother, amused by Vittorio's outburst.
I don't really mind sharing the same coach, Barbara
thought. Maybe I'll see him again, that way. She shook her
head in wonderment. That makes it two cute boys I've met
since I've been here!

Chapter Eight

*T*he little blue traveling clock on Barbara's night table started to ring at the stroke of seven. Barbara awoke, shut her eyes tightly against the noise, then reached out to turn it off, wondering sleepily why her mother had not yet wakened her.

Abruptly she sat up. Seven o'clock! I should have been on the rink an hour ago, she thought anxiously. Then she realized it was Sunday and that she had set the alarm herself the night before in order to meet Fiammetta and Neil and go exploring.

She flopped back onto her pillow, wishing she didn't have to get up just yet. Since she had last seen Neil at the beginning of the week, the days had been crowded with intensive skating and visits to the doctor who was caring for her long-neglected heel. Only the promise that she would soak it several hours a day had made him relent from his threat to stop her skating. Luckily the care had paid off.

A long, lazy morning in bed would be a welcome change, she thought, stretching. A crack of inviting sunlight appeared between the wooden shutters at her window. Barbara got up and peered through them, smiling at the now familiar peaks and the cloudless sky. I hope it stays that way, she thought. She had quickly learned that in the mountains a brilliant morning sky could often turn cloudy by noon and had therefore not objected when Neil had set eight o'clock as their meeting time.

The scene below her was filled with such quiet beauty that she wanted to linger at the window. An elderly gardener was wandering from a bed of red geraniums to one of orange nasturtiums, carrying a large watering can. Barbara noticed how gingerly he stepped on the graveled paths, as if trying not to disturb the sleeping hotel. From the garden, her eyes strayed to the tennis court, where a sunburned boy was pulling a massive roller over the rich terracotta clay. On the open terrace, waiters were in the process of dusting the scatter of white iron chairs and setting the tables for breakfast.

Ordinarily, Barbara enjoyed the luxury of having breakfast rolled into her room on a spanking white table, but today the look of sunlight on the terrace had great appeal, and she came away quickly from the window to get dressed and go downstairs.

By eight o'clock she was walking toward the village square, gray wool slacks and a warm blue cardigan keeping her snug against the morning chill. Neil was already waiting, a smile of welcome on his rugged face, and, as Barbara started to ask him about his exploits of the past week, Fiammetta joined them. She looked trim and elegant in a green wool pleated skirt, yet she threw an envious look in Barbara's direction, saying, "Now that's a sensible outfit for the mountains! I've never been able to convince my parents that slacks are considered quite ladylike under certain circumstances. I'm allowed to wear pants for skiing and rock climbing, and that's it!"

56

Neil looked from one to the other, amused. "Now, if you young ladies will stop discussing fashions, we might be on our way. We have a good bit of walking to do on the main road before we hit the trail, and it might be nice to get that over with before the traffic gets heavy."

They set out, walking briskly and continuing their conversation. Here and there a sunburned farmer, dressed in his Sunday clothes, tipped his hat and said *buon giorno* as he made his way toward one of the little churches in the village. A hay cart loaded with scrubbed-looking children clattered past them. The father, whip in hand, sat in the front seat holding the reins. His wife was resplendent in a flowered and fringed black skirt, and grandmother sat between them, a black shawl wrapped around her wrinkled face.

"I wish they were going our way. I'd love to ride in a hay wagon," Barbara said as she waved to them.

"They look pretty well filled up," Neil replied, "but perhaps, if you want to save your strength for the real hike, some car would pick us up."

He held his thumb out as a car whizzed by them on the curving road.

"Oh, I don't know," Barbara hesitated, "I'd never do that at home."

"I wouldn't either, if I were alone," Fiammetta added, "but since we are three, I'm sure it's all right. People always give rides to young hikers."

And a few seconds later, a small Fiat stopped alongside them, and a dark-haired child inquired if they wanted to be driven somewhere.

"Would you have enough room to take us to Falzarego?" Neil asked in his slow but understandable Italian. "If you don't mind being a little crowded," the man behind the wheel replied. "It's right on our way."

Neil sat in the front with the parents, and the two girls slid into the back seat next to the children, who immediately began asking them where they were going. Fiammetta explained that they were on their way to a mountain called *Le Cinque Torri* because it was a beautiful but not overly difficult hike, and they were introducing their American friend to the Dolomite mountains.

Barbara saw Fiammetta point toward a nest of baskets on the floor of the car and thought she understood her to ask if the family were going to pick strawberries. The involved reply was too much for Barbara, however, and Fiammetta explained that they were actually going mushrooming, or at least the parents were, but the two children preferred to hunt for berries.

"How would you know not to pick toadstools instead?" Barbara whispered to her friend. "And what do they do with the mushrooms anyway? Sell them?"

"I doubt that. They probably just like to eat them. They are quite delicious, you know. But you do have to know the different varieties: most of us learn as children. I used to love hunting for mushrooms in the woods, when I was small: the dank smell of the forest, and the quiet, and walking over moss and pine needles."

The road climbed steadily, and soon the meadows and potato fields of the valley gave way to pine woods and rocky ledges. Everywhere wild flowers brightened the landscape with patches of vibrant colors: tiny pink carnations perched on the banks of the road, clumps of bluebells, thousands of purple mountain orchids covering the occasional marshy areas. Then they reached a plateau, and the car stopped between a small hotel and a souvenir stand. Neil and the two girls got out and thanked their driver, and after they had pulled away, with much waving from both parties, Fiammetta told Barbara that they had wished the Signorina Americana much joy on her first hiking tour through these beautiful mountains.

With his back to the road, Neil placed his hand under Barbara's elbow.

"*Le Cinque Torri*, the five towers, are in that direction," he told her, pointing straight ahead, "but you can't see them now because there are other peaks in the way. They are five outcroppings of rock which look like towers, and the smallest one is in favor as a training ground for people learning to climb rock . . . not that we'll do any of that today," he added.

"Well, what are we going to do then?" Barbara inquired as they set out. They walked single file on a narrow path through a plain covered by sparse grass. "I thought that was what we were going to do, climb."

Fiammetta, who was walking ahead of her, replied without stopping, "Oh, no, you can't do that without training and proper equipment. It's much too dangerous."

And from behind her Neil chimed in, "We're going to hike as far as the *rifugio* at the foot of the 'towers.' There'll be plenty of boulders for you to scramble over along the way, but to try climbing sheer rock with no experience would be like my trying to do fancy figures my first time on skates."

They walked along in silence for a while, Barbara keeping her eyes on the path to avoid tripping on the many loose rocks. The sound of tinkling bells made her look up, and she saw, surprisingly close, a dozen sleepy-eyed cows loitering in their way. Laughing, Fiammetta led the way around them.

The path climbed a small incline, and when they reached its summit they were able to see, way in the distance, the five towers that Neil had described.

"Oh, Fiammetta," Barbara exclaimed excitedly, "those must be the peaks I saw that very first day, when we took the cable car together!" She was delighted to have recognized the mountain. "They looked so much more graceful from way up there, though!"

"That's one reason I find mountains so fascinating," Neil joined in. "They change so according to one's perspective! And wait until you really get up close!"

They hiked steadily upward for an hour or more. As they came to a steep area, the path forked in two different directions. Neil, who by then had taken over the head of the line, started toward the right, then stopped and turned to Barbara.

"Are you tired? Would you like to rest a few minutes before we go on?"

Gratefully, Barbara nodded yes. She had found that she was slightly short of breath, and conversation came with some difficulty.

"Supposing you hadn't been here before," she began, after a few moments of sitting quietly on a sun-warmed rock, "how would you know which turn to take? It must be awfully easy to get lost. A lot of this looks much the same to me."

60

Fiammetta replied, "Haven't you noticed the markings along the path? Every so often a rock or a stump of wood is marked with yellow or red. Each hiking tour has a different color. They do fade from sun and rain, though. The Alpine clubs are supposed to take care of repainting the markings each season."

"Wouldn't you think," Neil moved from the rock to the grass, where he sprawled comfortably, chin on hands, "that the clubs would have a hard time keeping up with the job?"

Fiammetta nodded and went on to describe how few people really hiked anymore, now that cars were so prevalent.

Barbara's attention waned, and her gaze, wandering over the landscape, was caught by a patch of bright blue wild flowers nestled near a rocky ledge. She got to her feet and strolled over for a closer look.

"Oh, look at this fabulous color! I've just got to bring some of these to my mother. I'd love a skating costume exactly this shade!"

"Those are gentians," Fiammetta explained. "They are practically a symbol of the Alps, along with edelweiss and wild rhododendron. You're not really supposed to pick them, you know; they've become quite rare, and there's a law to safeguard them. Though I'm sure it's all right to take one or two," she added, not wanting to discourage her friend.

While Fiammetta talked, Barbara's hand reached out to pluck a blossom. A little farther into the grass she noticed a cone-shaped object. Wondering what it might be, she moved closer to it. It seemed embedded in the ground and with both hands she tried to free it.

"What are you doing over there?" Neil's voice came closer. "Find a buried treasure, did you?"

Suddenly he was behind her, and his voice grew sharp. "Leave that alone, right away!"

Annoyed at his bossiness, Barbara wheeled around. "Why, whatever is the matter!"

"Barbara, Barbara, take your hand away!" Fiammetta had joined them, and her face was filled with concern. "That's a cannon shell. You must never, never touch them! It's always possible that they might still be loaded!"

"What do you mean, a cannon shell?" Barbara looked at her friends, wondering if they were pulling her leg. "What would it be doing here? There hasn't been a war in twenty years!"

The Italian girl shook her head. "It's been here much longer than that. Shells like this one date back to the First World War, when so much of the fighting took place in these mountains."

"Have you ever found one? What do you do with them?"

"No, I haven't, but people find them all the time. You're supposed to leave them, and later notify the police of their location so they can come and detonate the shell."

They made careful note of where they had found it, Neil pacing off the distance between the shell and the rock where they had sat, and then took up their walk again. The terrain was getting steeper and rockier, and several times Barbara used her hands as well as her feet to get herself over an unusually large boulder. Neil and Fiammetta walked ahead of her, stopping to help her whenever they thought she might need it.

"I can't get that shell out of my head," Barbara said, wiping the dust off her slacks after a spill. "I was just trying to imagine what the fighting must have been like in these mountains, never knowing who was coming at you from where. Before this, I had never even thought of war as part of somebody's life."

"It was dreadful fighting, you're right. This whole area has never forgotten it." Fiammetta spoke earnestly.

"Never forgotten? How do you mean that?"

"Well, the legends, and the songs, many speak of the war. There is a flower that grows in the valley which is said to have sprung up wherever the blood of Italian soldiers was shed. And now, as we come around this mountain, I'll show you something else."

The path worked its way closely around the foot of a tall pinnacle. To the right of the path, the mountain fell away sharply in a field of loose stones, all but covered with small yellow poppies glowing in the midmorning sun. Stretched far below them was a lush green valley, a cluster of sheep moving slowly across it.

"Do you see that mountain over there, right across from us, at the other end of the valley?"

Barbara followed Fiammetta's finger. "Oh, you mean that one, that looks a little like a volcano? It isn't though, is it? I never heard of one in this part of the world."

"No, it certainly isn't. That was an ordinary mountain before its top was blown off during the First World War."

This time it was Neil's turn to look incredulous. "You really are improving our education today, Fiammetta. I never heard that tale. Why on earth was the mountain's top blown off?"

"There was an enemy patrol in hiding there, and it seemed the most complete way to get rid of it. They just dynamited the whole thing."

"And it doesn't look as though any vegetation ever grew back over it," Barbara added, turning to give the mountain one last look as they went on. And all the while they walked, she couldn't shake the sense of wonder at this wholly new world she seemed to be discovering.

By the time they came in sight of the *rifugio* the sun was high, and the two girls had removed their sweaters and tied them around their waists. Three hours of skating practice never tire me this much, Barbara thought, delighted to see the toylike brown chalet huddled against the side of a large rocky peak.

"That's the smallest of the *Cinque Torri*," Neil said, pointing to the cliff. "Doesn't it look different up close from what we saw before?"

They walked toward it across a wide green plain, side-stepping puddles in the marshy ground. Outside the chalet, a few people sat in the sun at rough brown tables, while some relaxed in low deck chairs in shirt-sleeves and halter tops.

The sound of singing reached through the open windows, and as they went through the door they almost collided with a wrinkled, white-haired woman carrying a large wooden board laden with something golden and steaming.

Neil inhaled blissfully. "Ah! *Polenta* and mountain singing! Why was I ever born an Englishman!"

Fiammetta laughed at his enthusiasm and suggested that they have their lunch out in the sun. Sinking happily into three rather hard chairs, sheltered from the wind by the walls of the house, they stretched their legs and turned their faces toward the sun.

Barbara saw the waitress coming in their direction and inquired quickly of Fiammetta, "What does one order here? I'm really famished after all that walking."

"They usually have one hot dish," Fiammetta explained, "and it's always a hearty one. It seems to be *polenta* today. It's like cornmeal, Barbara, served with meat or sausage, or just plain. It's the main staple around here, like spaghetti is farther south. I'm surprised they haven't served it at the hotel."

Barbara looked doubtful. "The hotel is very nice about cooking whatever we ask for, so we haven't really had to try anything new."

"Why Barbara, you're not as adventurous as I thought, then," Neil added only half in jest as he helped himself from a platter of plump brown sausages. The waitress then set down the wooden board next to Fiammetta, and Barbara was intrigued to watch her friend as she held a thin piece of white string taut with both hands and with it sliced thick pieces of the cornmeal for each of them.

Barbara poked her fork into it gingerly, then brought a small piece to her mouth.

"I do like it," she said, turning to Neil, "and you're probably right about my not being adventurous. I've never even wondered whether I am or not!"

But even while she said it, she realized that this day was as close as she had ever been to an adventure. I came to Europe to skate, she thought. Just to skate. It certainly is turning out differently from what I had expected!

She dug more courageously into her food.

The scraping of many chairs announced the end of lunch for the large group that had been bursting into occasional song. A dozen men and women, heavy mountain boots clumping on the wooden floor, filed out into the sunshine and sat on the grass, followed closely by the elderly waitress who poured each of them a cup of black steaming coffee. A tall, stout gentleman started to hum, and presently voices all around joined in a rather nostalgic melody.

Neil set down his knife and fork, leaned back in the chair and added his resonant voice to the chorus.

Fiammetta, in answer to Barbara's questioning glance, explained in a whisper, "It's called '*La Montanara*,' the mountain song, and it's been a favorite for years with Italian hikers. It's almost their theme song."

"It's a beautiful tune," Barbara replied softly. "I'd love to learn the words to it."

It had a slow, melancholy melody, and Barbara could see herself skating to it in a gentian blue costume. Fiammetta sang the words clearly in her direction, promising to translate them later, and Barbara strained to catch as much of the meaning as she could:

> *Là su per le montagne,*
> *tra boschi e valli d'or,*
> *fra l'aspre rupi echeggia*
> *un cantico d'amore.*
>
> *'La montanara, ohè'*
> *si sente cantare,*
> *'cantiam la montanara*
> *e chi non la sa?'*

The singing stopped, and while the group arose and walked back into the *rifugio*, Fiammetta told Barbara the meaning of the words.

> *High up in the mountains*
> *amidst forests and golden valleys*
> *a song of love echoes*
> *from the rugged peaks.*
>
> *It is 'La Montanara'*
> *that everyone is singing,*
> *let us sing 'La Montanara'*
> *for who knows it not?*

A few moments later, the tall gentleman who had led the singing emerged again, followed by a short, wiry, gray-haired man with deep crevices in his sunburned face. He wore a red parka with an emblem picturing a squirrel on his arm, and a large coil of rope was slung over his shoulder. A young boy came running out after them, and together they disappeared down a trail which started behind the chalet.

"Now *they*," Neil explained, "are going climbing, as distinct from hiking. You may have noticed that they carried a rope. The man in red is a guide, and my guess is that he's taking them up the smallest of the 'towers.' "

"Do you suppose we could watch them? I'd really love to see how it's done, if it's not too far," Barbara asked eagerly.

Fifteen minutes later the three of them were sitting on soft moss at the very base of the novice climb. Seen from any distance, the peak might have seemed smooth and slippery. Yet as Barbara sat below it, head thrown back, she could see all the small imperfections, the holds and points and ledges on which climbers could place their feet. Several groups could be seen at various levels of the mountain, looking to Barbara like pictures glued to a montage. Their voices were surprisingly clear even from the very top, as the sound carried down the mountain.

Here and there, a few other spectators had gathered to watch the proceedings on the side of the cliff. Two young girls were halfway up the peak, with a rope around their waists, and they seemed uncertain as to what their next step should be. The guide could be heard shouting instructions to them in pidgin French.

"Now I see why you told me that you sometimes go along with your father as an interpreter," Barbara said to her friend. "Do you actually have to go on the climb, or can you shout from below?"

"I usually climb too. Most of the ascents people make are longer than this one, and you can't always be heard clearly enough by shouting."

"It certainly looks challenging." Barbara was filled with excitement. "Would you trust me to come along with you on a Sunday when I didn't have to skate?"

The question was directed at Neil, and both he and Fiammetta nodded.

"Oh, I think you'd be safe enough with the two of us; we're both fairly experienced!" Neil was making fun of her, but his grin was quite disarming. "I'll put myself in charge of looking out for your precious ankles. And incidentally," he added, "I think we'd better get you back to the hotel now, or tomorrow you might be too tired for pirouetting on the ice!"

Her legs were tired, indeed, and so was the rest of her, Barbara realized as they approached Fiammetta's house late in the afternoon. The Bianchis' home was first on the way back, and Barbara and Neil had accepted gladly Fiammetta's invitation to stop in and meet her parents.

As they came up to the front door, they could hear a male voice shouting at an angry pitch. Fiammetta looked up at the open window behind the wooden balcony which surrounded the house.

"That sounds like Zio Vittorio," she said, frowning.

They heard a woman reply, her voice unsteady with the attempt to fight down tears.

"I'm afraid it doesn't seem like a good time for introductions," Fiammetta said in embarrassment. "In fact, I think I'd better go right up and see what is going on!"

"I'll see you tomorrow," Barbara called after her. "I hope nothing's wrong."

Then she and Neil continued toward the center of town.

Chapter Nine

*B*arbara tied the ribbon on her white cuddle cap securely under her chin. She inhaled the sharp, cold morning air, then walked across the wooden planking to the ice.

She had expected to be the first one there, but at that very moment the rink was the setting for an intricate performance by Fiammetta and her uncle.

Vittorio was holding Fiammetta's arms and swinging her around and around in a spinning whirl, then Fiammetta, in a spectacular leap, was sitting on his shoulder, her arms upraised.

Barbara applauded and sang out a rousing fanfare. Then, puzzled, she asked, "Hey, teacher, look here! That was very impressive and all that, but how about the skating rule book? You know . . . that section on 'forbidden movements'? Isn't there something about not carrying your partner on your shoulders?"

Vittorio was about to answer, but Fiammetta interrupted him.

"Oh, Barbara, wait until you hear! The Ice Revue is coming to Cortina this weekend, and they are holding auditions on Friday! Zio Vittorio has been helping me work out a routine. I'm so nervous I don't even know what I'm saying!"

Barbara gave her friend a warm hug. "So that's what you were doing! Isn't that wonderful news! And have your parents agreed to your trying out, then?"

Their coach smiled and flicked an imaginary bit of dust off his navy blue blazer. "Well, I spent most of yesterday afternoon arguing with my brother, and especially my sister-in-law. But by the time you returned from your hike, I had them quite convinced."

Barbara cocked her head. "Oh, is that what we heard through the window as we were coming back? Your persuasive powers?"

Vittorio was about to light his cigar, and he looked up sheepishly before blowing out his match.

"Ah, yes! I suppose I did get a bit overheated toward the end. I might have never convinced them if I hadn't been able to suggest that you and your mother would keep an eye on their little girl if she goes to the United States!"

"But first, I have to win the audition," Fiammetta shook her blond head doubtfully. "And I have so little time to practice. I don't dare quit my job until I know if I'm accepted!"

Barbara lightly touched her on the shoulder. "I'll be glad to help you whenever you're free to practice. If you need a partner, that is. Although there's an awful lot I don't know about professional skating!"

The three of them skated toward the edge of the arena and sat down on one of the benches.

"You can certainly help her with figures, Barbara," Vittorio said. "They are just as basic to a professional routine as to an amateur. It's only in pair skating that there is a real difference," he continued. "That's where you find all those jumps and movements which are constantly used in shows and carnivals but which are taboo by amateur standards."

He put an arm around both their shoulders. "I'm not really worried about you, Fiammetta. I'm quite sure you'll be accepted, but work out whenever you can, anyway. Just keep in mind that they'll be watching your grace and your carriage, and don't worry."

But worry she did, and Barbara was kept fully occupied between her own skating pursuits and those of her friend.

Friday came faster than either of them would have thought possible. At eight-thirty Barbara and her mother were in their seats at the stadium, watching the entrances for Fiammetta and her family, who were due to join them.

The first performance of the Ice Revue was about to begin, and Fiammetta had auditioned that very afternoon. The rows of seats were alive with elegant spectators, eagerly peering down at the brightly lit ice.

Barbara caught a glimpse of her friend walking up the steps toward them and got up quickly to let her pass.

"How was the audition? What did they say? Are you coming back to the States with us?" She was so impatient to hear about the audition that how-do-you-dos to Mr. and Mrs. Bianchi were all but forgotten.

"I don't know yet. I don't think I made any mistakes, and they didn't ask for anything very difficult. The manager said he would let me know, but he said the same thing to the girl before me."

Fiammetta had just enough time to introduce her parents before the lights dimmed.

When the ice was darkened, a spotlight suddenly illuminated a portly, gray-haired gentleman who looked incongruous in skates and a dinner jacket.

Fiammetta nudged Barbara, whispering, "That's the man who auditioned me this afternoon."

"*Buona sera, Signore e Signori.*"

Barbara smiled at his 'good evening,' realizing that the Italian words had obviously been learned for the occasion.

"We are very pleased to be performing in your beautiful Olympic Stadium."

He spoke slowly, and with some difficulty, and Barbara found that by listening carefully she was able to understand most of the words.

"We are also very happy to announce," the manager continued, "that starting next month, our company will be joined by a talented young skater from your enchanting town, Signorina Fiammetta Bianchi."

The opening number was completely lost to the two girls in their joy over this announcement. With a happy squeal, Barbara and Fiammetta threw their arms around each other, immediately attracting the attention of spectators nearby. Here and there, stares of annoyance turned to smiles of recognition. Finally, Vittorio shushed them and they settled down to watch the performance.

Two clowns dressed as cleaning women, one a skinny beanpole and the other short and very round, hobbled in awkwardly on their skates, weighed down by pails and mops. Immediately they tripped each other, and then began a wild chase with mops flying, buckets of water narrowly missing aim, skates practically grazing the prostrate body of a fallen clown. In retaliation, the egg-shaped one arose and, in great anger, picked up his enemy and dumped him in a bucket, setting it spinning with a forceful push. Around and around the rink the bucket whirled, the tall clown waving this way and that, arms flailing in a desperate attempt to keep his balance. As he came around each bend, shrieks went up from the spectators who thought surely he would spill out on top of them. At last the pail lost momentum and slowed to a stop. The bogus cleaning woman reached down to grasp the sides of the bucket, then, to the surprise of the audience, pulled it up over his head, revealing that it had no bottom.

Barbara, impressed with the clown's performance, turned to Fiammetta and still giggling said, "Wasn't that fabulous skating?"

Fiammetta nodded smiling. "I really thought he was in a bucket that was gliding around on the ice. Just think how good a skater one has to be to turn it all into a comedy!"

Before Barbara could answer, the ice was given over to a line of Scottish lassies in brilliant plaids, down to the spats on their white skates. They formed a circle, then a star, then they played a perfectly timed version of crack-the-whip. The steps were elementary, but the girls were all pretty, wore uniformly dazzling smiles and performed in flawless formation. They drew enthusiastic applause from the audience.

Well, now, wasn't that a lot of nothing, thought Barbara during the performance.

"Did you see how simple their moves were?" she asked Fiammetta as they walked down the aisle at intermission time. "No wonder they were happy to have you! You're a much better skater than anyone in that chorus line." While

Fiammetta walked ahead, she went on, unthinking. "Aren't you going to find it dull very quickly? You'll be skating the same old steps; the only change will be in the costumes."

Fiammetta turned her head with a radiant smile. "What were you saying? The costumes? They were lovely, weren't they? Why, I bet I'll have more clothes than I've ever had in my life!"

At once, Barbara was ashamed of her prattling and glad that Fiammetta had not really heard her.

They all sat together at the coffee shop. Vittorio acted as interpreter for Mrs. McAllister, while she reassured Fiammetta's parents that she would be happy to look after their daughter when she reached the United States.

Mr. Bianchi, a slightly taller and more weather-beaten version of Vittorio, was visibly proud of his daughter's achievement, but Mrs. Bianchi could not hide her nervousness. She asked thousands of questions about the trip, the traffic in New York, the habits of American girls. Who would nurse Fiammetta when she caught cold from wearing such scanty costumes on the ice, Mrs. Bianchi wondered unhappily.

Fiammetta's cheeks deepened by several shades as she tried vainly to steer her mother's conversation away from the subject. Mrs. McAllister's comforting words, heartily seconded by Barbara, eventually seemed to relax Mrs. Bianchi. It was agreed that Fiammetta would fly home with them, and that she would stay at their apartment whenever the Ice Revue appeared in New York City.

As they started toward their seats again, Barbara heard a voice behind them calling her Miss McAllister. She turned to find herself face to face with Dario Visconti, who bowed low over her hand.

"I assume this is the young lady who will join the Ice Revue," he smiled at Fiammetta before Barbara had a chance to introduce him, "since I saw you two overcome with joy when the announcement was made."

Barbara nodded happily and made introductions all around.

"Would you all do me the honor of joining me after the performance to drink to the good health of our celebrity?" Unmistakably, though the invitation was issued to everyone present, his gaze rested on Barbara, and she was crushed to hear Vittorio beat out without hesitation, "I'm afraid not. Both these young ladies have a great deal of practicing to do over the next few weeks, and they need as much sleep as they can get."

Embarrassed, Barbara put in hurriedly, "I have an idea. Fiammetta and I are going mountain climbing with an English friend of ours on Sunday. Would you like to join us, Dario?"

Poised as ever, he threw a charming smile in her direction.

"Not exactly what I would suggest as a way to spend Sunday with two young ladies, but since your free time is so limited, I'm at your command."

He moved gracefully among the older generation, saying good-bye, then turned to the two girls and said, "Shall I meet you Sunday morning in the lobby of the hotel? About ten?"

"Oh, no," Fiammetta exploded. "We can't start in the

middle of the day! I'm sure Neil will want to leave by eight at the very latest!"

Dario shrugged lazily, saluted with his hand and turned toward Barbara. "I'll call you tomorrow to hear what time reveille is to be."

He left them as the lights began to dim, and if Fiammetta had any doubts she wanted to voice, there was no time left to express them as the second half of the ice show swung into being.

Chapter Ten

*F*iammetta was ready and waiting outside her house as Dario's white Cadillac drove up for her. From the back seat, Barbara opened the car door, and beckoned to her friend to sit beside her.

Boy, am I ever glad to have her along, Barbara thought as she slid over to make room. Dario and Neil have been snapping at each other ever since I introduced them in the hotel lobby. It hadn't occurred to me that Neil would resent Dario's joining us, but he certainly seems to!

"Good morning Barbara, Neil, Dario," Fiammetta said as she settled into her seat, quite unaware of the tensions around her. "I brought my extra climbing boots along for you, Barbara. I think they will fit. What a beautiful car this is, Dario. I've never ridden in an American car before. We don't see very many of them around here."

"And rightly so," Neil muttered under his breath.

Dario laughed. "Are you worried about my car? I assure you I can handle these roads just as well as you can!" He backed out of Fiammetta's driveway and turned to Neil on his right. "Where to, leader? I have not been informed of our destination!"

Neil looked up, sensing the sarcasm in his voice. "I thought we'd go back to where we hiked the last time and let Barbara practice climbing *Le Cinque Torri*. I take it you have climbed before?"

"You forget I was born but three hours from here. These mountains are nothing new to me, you know. I'm not as much in awe of them as you seem to be. In fact," he turned to look at Barbara for confirmation, "I think it's childish to go on such a beginner's climb. Barbara is a trained athlete, after all. I'm sure she can keep up with you."

"Yes, Neil, I agree." Barbara felt flattered by Dario's remarks. "Why go back to a mountain we've already seen? I'd much rather try something new."

"Barbara, I think you should let Neil decide." Fiammetta's voice was serious.

"Your first attempt should be on an easy slope," Neil added.

"Where there are plenty of other people around," Fiammetta continued.

"Just listen to the old folks!" Dario mocked.

Barbara placed a hand on Neil's shoulder. "Oh, come on, Neil. You promised me an adventure! I train all the time; let's not make this just another lesson!"

Neil looked at her over his shoulder and smiled at the eager expression on her face. Barbara's blue eyes sparkled with intensity; the red sweater seemed to be reflected in her glowing cheeks.

"Is this how you get what you want? All right, athlete, we won't go where it's beneath your dignity!" He turned toward his left. "Dario, let us set forth in your white charger and head toward Misurina. I've climbed some magnificent mountains near there in the last few weeks."

Whew! Barbara thought. Everything's an argument today! It began as early as seven-thirty this morning, when Mother woke up complaining that she had worried all night about my going mountain climbing.

"Why, honestly, Mother, I don't understand you," Barbara had replied, standing by the tall wardrobe with her gray slacks over her arm. "You know me; I wouldn't try something I couldn't handle! And it's not as if I were going with inexperienced people!"

She had been shocked by her mother's reluctance to let her try something new. Suddenly, a real yearning had welled up inside her to shake loose from her own routine, to explore someone else's world. She could hardly wait to get started!

Eagerly now she reached toward the floor of the car for the boots which Fiammetta had brought her, examining the thick rubber soles which looked like the treads of automobile tires. She slipped off her own loafers and grimaced at the awkward picture that her feet made in their climbing gear.

"Stop making faces," Fiammetta said, laughing. "I gave you my newer boots. Look at the antiques I'm wearing!" And she swung her foot up to show the hob nails sticking out of the soles of her heavy leather boots.

Dario peered into the rear view mirror at the two girls and let out an incredulous laugh. "We're not scaling Mt. Everest today, are we? Personally, I prefer wearing tennis shoes. And what are you doing, playing around with that rope?" he questioned Neil sarcastically.

Neil, a thick coil of rope spread across his knees, was carefully slipping it through his fingers inch by inch. He stopped just long enough to throw his neighbor a disgruntled look.

His tone was cold. "It's important to check the rope before you use it, or didn't you know? It might have just the smallest cut in it, and I imagine I don't have to tell you what *that* could do."

Dario snorted and with a shrug dismissed the matter. Bending low over the wheel, he skillfully drove his long automobile around hairpin curves and up and down steep inclines. At each turn in the road a new vista stretched out before them; deep green pine trees throwing their jagged shadows across emerald fields, shimmering torrents now rushing down steep ravines, now winding peacefully through a valley far below the roadside. High above them, each ridge of white-crowned mountain gave way to another, shell-pink in the morning sunshine. Soon they were driving along the vast lake of Misurina, admiring the startling reflection of two hotels, encircled by snowy pinnacles.

They turned off the highway, and the road became steeper and poorly surfaced. The endless succession of sharp curves kept throwing the two girls against each other, and the sheer drop visible from Barbara's side of the car made her want to look away. Unperturbed, Dario kept on, clucking in mock sympathy at a stalled car, its driver raising the hood to let the engine cool.

At a narrow part of the road, a car coming down the mountain was forced to back up a few feet to make room for the girth of their own vehicle. Barbara's laughter mingled with Dario's at the soundless oaths they saw the driver utter. In a moment, the road had ended, and they parked their car on the rim of a wide plateau.

Barbara welcomed the rush of cold air as she opened the door, for she had begun to feel quite queasy during the last few minutes. Gladly she stepped outside. Up here all the colors were muted, from the straggly, almost gray grass of the plateau on which she stood to the many shades of the rock which surrounded them. Gone were the lush greens of the vistas in the valley. The timber line was well below them, and Barbara felt excited and stimulated by the chill air and the feeling of height.

"Which way do we go, Neil? Where do we start climbing?"

Neil had just stepped out of the car, and he came toward her, the very picture of a mountain climber in his khaki knee breeches and beige turtleneck sweater, buckling the straps of his knapsack as he walked. He took her arm and led her to a narrow path which hugged the side of the pinnacle they were to climb.

Fiammetta, also wearing knee breeches, followed alongside Dario.

Barbara turned her head to look at Dario's carefully pressed blue jeans, and she commented in surprise, "I never thought to bring my dungarees. I wouldn't have expected them to be respectable in Europe. I guess they must be, though, if you're wearing them!"

Before Dario had a chance to reply, Neil cut in with a sharp, "Oh, they're all the rage among the young fashionables of Italy! They go with American cars and the latest in dances!"

82

Dario's face angered, and he walked faster to catch up with Neil and reply to him in kind. Neil, realizing that Fiammetta had fallen behind, strode briskly toward her, cheating Dario of his chance to trade insults. Dario shrugged. He leaned toward Barbara and whispered, his lips nearly brushing her face, "Those two really belong together, don't they? They are both . . . what is that word you use . . . so . . . square?"

Their closeness lasted only a second, but Barbara felt troubled by it. She was torn between Dario and her other friends, and obviously they were not going to get along. Before she had time to think further, Dario took her hand and started down the rocky path at a brisk run, pulling her after him.

"Come on, let's get away from them!" he called over his shoulder, laughing at her bewildered face.

Spurred by his enthusiasm, her feet bouncing along on the springy rubber soles of her boots, Barbara gave herself up to the joy of the unexpected race.

A little farther on, rounding a sharp bend, they had to stop abruptly as a middle-aged couple in mountaineer attire passed them on the narrow path. The woman smiled at the near-collision, stopped, and spoke a few words in rapid Italian, indicating a small bouquet of grayish flowers tied to the opening of her knapsack.

"What did she say?" Barbara wanted to know from Dario as the couple walked briskly on.

"They found some edelweiss, and she just had to let us know! It's supposed to be quite an achievement, you know!" He resumed walking, but Barbara sat down on a rock.

"Let's wait here, Dario. We've gotten too far from the others. Besides, I want to know more about the edelweiss. Why are they so special? They're not really pretty!"

Dario came back a few paces and sat on the grass at her feet, resting his chin on his drawn up knees. "They only grow on the highest ledges, and they seem to have become a symbol of the unattainable. But I shall risk my life to find one for you, if you wish it." With these words, Dario fell on one knee, his hand on his heart and a smitten expression on his catlike face.

Barbara was laughing delightedly when Neil and Fiammetta caught up with them. Neil shot them a disapproving glance and said in a businesslike tone, "Are you ready for the climb? The approach is just a few hundred yards from here."

Barbara jumped to her feet, embarrassed. "Oh, let's go! Are you going to tie us all up with your rope?"

"We probably should," Fiammetta interjected grinning, "just so you won't run away again."

"Well, I'm not going to 'tie' you 'up' yet, as you put it. First we're going to have to make our way up that scree."

They scrambled up the steep incline of rock fragments which led to the base of the pinnacle they were to climb. Once Barbara slipped, feeling the rough stones slide out from under her feet. As she regained her balance, she saw, out of the corner of her eye, a grimace of pain on Dario's face.

"Oh, Dario! You really shouldn't have worn those sneakers. You must be feeling every stone!"

His expression changed to annoyance, and she wished

84

she had not spoken out loud. I guess he doesn't want any weakness to show, she thought.

In a short while they caught up with Neil, who was waiting for them at the foot of the peak. He handed each of them a separate length of rope, and showed Barbara how to pass it five or six times around her waist, tying the ends with a complicated knot. A metal snap link was then clipped on to the coils at her waist. To the link, Neil attached the long climbing rope that would join the four of them together.

Head thrown back, Barbara scrutinized the mountain they would soon attempt. Now that she was close enough to touch the face of the mountain, she could see a variety of tiny ledges and cracks to use as footholds.

"I'm going first, Barbara," Neil said, swinging the coil of rope diagonally across his chest. "When I reach a good ledge, I'll belay the rope—tie it to a strong hold, that is—and then you'll come up. Then Fiammetta, and Dario next. Watch me as I go up, and use the same holds. And remember not to move from one position until you've looked carefully where you're going to put your feet next. And don't forget to pay out your rope as I go up."

Barbara had been watching him with such intense concentration that he had to smile.

"All right, Champ," he gave her shoulder an encouraging pat, "show us what you can do!"

With that, he placed his right foot onto a small in-pocket in the stone; his left hand found a shelf above his head, and then up came the left foot. There was no hesitation as one foot after the other went up to a higher hold, his hands seeming to rest lightly on the rocks, his body in perfect balance.

He's as effortless as a squirrel in Central Park, Barbara thought as she paid out some of the rope between her fingers. Fiammetta came up close behind her and said, "Watch him now. He'll be swinging himself up over the ledge in another minute, and then it'll be your turn to start. Do be careful, Barbara. Remember not to move from one position until you've made certain where you'll put your feet next."

Dario snorted and shook his head in dismay. "The way you and Neil carry on over a simple climb, it's really unbelievable."

Barbara was filled with growing excitement, and she happily threw her arms around Fiammetta. "Don't worry, I'll live to tell my skating pals about the adventure. I think I've memorized every foot and hand hold Neil used!"

She looked up to see Neil disappear for a moment over the edge of a small plateau. She could feel the rope being pulled taut against the face of the mountain; then he came into view, standing fully upright. "All right, Barbara. Up you come." His voice carried as clearly as if he were near to her.

She slipped on her gloves and placed her foot eagerly on the first hold. Her mind saw a map of the exact route Neil followed, and now she found the same nicks and ruts, bumps and flakes, as she made her way up. The rock itself was all she really saw, and she was surprised to find the point of Neil's boot directly overhead in what seemed like mere seconds. His hand was stretched out toward her, but Barbara shook her head determinedly and hoisted herself onto the flat ledge. In a sitting position, she leaned back on her hands and slid backward until her shoulders touched the rock, then she closed her eyes and sighed contentedly.

"Oh, that was wonderful fun, Neil! It wasn't difficult at all! And it's so lovely sitting here in the sun!"

Neil, squatting at the edge, called down to Fiammetta to start her climb. Then he turned, smiling, to Barbara.

"You did very well, except that you came up a bit too fast. If it had been a longer ascent, you'd have been winded long before the end. Come and watch Fiammetta. See how easy she takes it?"

Barbara crouched beside him, peering over the edge. She could see the top of a blond head moving slowly but unhesitatingly upward. She leaned out a bit farther to catch a glimpse of Dario at the foot of the pinnacle. Seeing the side of the mountain from that angle, and the steep scree falling away from the base, made Barbara feel suspended in space, her head spinning. She drew back quickly against the mountain, forcing her eyes to focus on the rope which Neil had belayed onto a knob in the rock just above them.

Careful not to mention her dizziness, she smiled a greeting at Fiammetta, and together they waited for Dario to come up. Neil turned around, laugh lines crinkling at the side of his eyes.

"I must say I'm tempted to let the rope go! But that would hardly be proper behavior for a guest in a foreign country!"

Why do they dislike each other so much, Barbara wondered for the hundredth time that day. And why do they keep telling *me* about it? Could it be because . . . could it be *because* of me?

She felt herself blushing at the idea. Quickly, to hide her

87

embarrassment, she took up Neil's ironic mood, and replied to his remark, "No, no, don't let the rope go! You don't like driving American cars, so how would we ever get back to Cortina!"

Fiammetta looked reproachful. "Don't talk that way, even in fun! I keep worrying that he may slip, climbing so fast and in his tennis shoes!"

But Dario made it as easily as the others, and he had no sooner joined them than he was ready for more.

"I hadn't really thought of going any farther," Neil replied, looking to Barbara for her reaction. "No point in getting Barbara too tired on her first try. She still has the descent to tackle."

Dario blew out a match and tossed it indignantly into the sky.

"Surely you didn't have us come all the way out here just to climb to the first ledge! Let's at least get to the top of this peak!"

Barbara bent her neck back to scale the mountain with her eyes.

"I can't tell where this pinnacle ends and the next begins, but I'm not at all tired. Do let's go on!"

The rib that led to the top of the peak was somewhat more difficult to master. To Barbara, the rock felt much smoother, and there were fewer cracks to hold on to, so she shifted her weight more slowly, growing increasingly aware of the vast space below her. This time, she gratefully accepted Neil's hand and let him help her onto the narrow ledge on which he stood.

It was a strangely satisfying feeling to stand on the very

summit, with taller mountains a short distance away, crowned with white snow. Way below them, at the mouth of the valley, she could see the spiraling road on which they had driven. A shiver of excitement went through her, and she hugged her shoulders.

"It is chilly up here, isn't it?" Neil said. "We won't stay long, Barbara. We'll be ready to start down as soon as the other two get here."

When they were ready to descend, Dario insisted on being first. With a cocky salute to Barbara, he swung his legs over the rim of the ledge.

"Don't forget to pay out the rope after me," he called to her. "Remember, now, my life is in your hands!"

As they waited for Dario to reach the first stopping point, Neil double-checked the rope around Barbara's waist. He briefed her on the descent, telling her to step down sideways whenever possible. Then Dario yelled up that he was ready, and Barbara sat down on the edge, in order to lower herself.

She looked below. Suddenly the side of the mountain looked to her like a tower of ice, slippery and treacherous, and quite devoid of footholds. For a second she hesitated. She saw that Fiammetta was reading her thoughts, and she stiffened. Nonsense, she told herself. That's exactly the way you came up. The footholds are there, even though they may be harder to see from above.

She started down, her eyes searching out cracks in the rock slab. She lowered herself to the first crag, then stood, one hand grasping a flake of rock, her body sideways, almost brushing the face of the mountain. She planned her next move, careful not to look much farther down than necessary, yet anxious to know how far she'd have to go before reaching the ledge on which Dario was waiting.

Slowly, carefully, Barbara made her way a little farther. She planted her feet firmly on an incut pocket, holding on with her hands, and looked down, her eyes hunting for Dario. Surely by now, she thought, she must be coming close to the place where he was waiting. Yet all that was visible was the rope. It seemed to be curving around the side of a boulder.

Mystified, Barbara continued her descent, stretching her foot toward a nick in the rock. Before her foot was entirely settled, she shifted her weight on to it and lowered the other leg. And then she slipped.

For an eternity she felt her arms flailing in the air and her hands hopelessly clawing at the surface of the mountain. In the same instant, the sky, the valley below and all the air around her seemed filled with the sound of a piercing wind, gone the moment it came. Or was it her own voice screaming? She could feel nothing but empty space.

Suddenly, there was a brutal tug of the rope around her waist. She could hear Neil's reassuring voice, and as he called to her, Barbara found the notches on which to rest her hands and anchor her feet. She lowered herself a bit farther until Neil ordered her to wait where she was.

Heart thudding and cheeks aflame, Barbara sank down, exhausted, upon a small platform of rock. She closed her eyes and huddled against the side of the mountain, hands clasping the rope around her waist. If it hadn't been for that, she thought numbly. If it hadn't been for that.

Dario's voice startled her. "Look what I brought you!"

Slowly she turned to face him. "Where were you? Didn't you hear me scream? Why weren't you waiting for me? I couldn't see you anywhere!" Her voice rose uncontrollably.

"Barbara, what's wrong? I saw some edelweiss behind that boulder, and I knew you'd like to have them! So I went to get them. Were you frightened?"

She looked, dazed, at the small gray bouquet in his outstretched hand, at the ingratiating smile on his lips. You knew I'd like to have them, she repeated in her mind. You'd do anything for me, wouldn't you? Anything, except what is really needed. I needed you where you were supposed to be, we all needed you. And you weren't there. You let us all down.

Not until much later, when she was resting on her bed, back at the hotel, was Barbara able to sort out what seemed to her, drowsy and bone weary as she was, a Revelation on the Mountain. She smiled self-consciously at the lofty phrase, then Neil's face came into her thoughts. He had been full of concern and gentleness when he had reached her on the ledge. He could have been, and well she knew it, hopping mad that she had insisted on going too far. Instead, he had reviewed the instructions for the last, brief part of the descent, talking to her in soft, reassuring tones. He had insisted that Fiammetta climb down alongside her, while he remained above them, stoutly belaying both their ropes. And as soon as they all had their feet on the scree again, he had taken Barbara's hand and kept it in his until they had walked all the way to the car.

Now, unable to fight off sleep, it seemed to her that several times during the long hike back she had felt an understanding pressure on her fingers.

Dario wasn't concerned with anyone's safety . . . he just wanted to make a grand gesture, to show off. And as for me, she thought drowsily, I've never cared about anything except my own success, be it skating or climbing too high a mountain. Yet Neil and Fiammetta are different. They've always sensed what I think the rope taught me today—that you can't climb to any heights alone.

Chapter Eleven

Mrs. McAllister's gaze was on her daughter as Barbara slowly opened her eyes. She blinked, surprised to find her mother in bed.

"What time is it? You weren't here when I got home, so I thought I'd have a nap until dinner time."

"It's morning, Barbara. You were sleeping so soundly when I got back yesterday afternoon, I figured you needed rest more than dinner. That must have been quite an exhausting hike!"

Why, that's right, thought Barbara, I'm still in my clothes!

"I did see Dario in the dining room," Mrs. McAllister continued, as she sat up and slipped into her bathrobe. "He wasn't too talkative about your excursion, though. Was it fun?"

Barbara threw back her quilt and got up abruptly, feeling an ache in her arms and shoulders.

"Where were you when we got back?" she asked, reluctant to reply to her mother's question. And then, to change the subject, "Ouch! I'm sore all over! I sure could have used a massage!"

A look of annoyance passed over Mrs. McAllister's face.

"I was busy, Barbara, and on *your* business!" She turned away and headed for the telephone. "Let me order breakfast first. Then I'll tell you all about where I was when you got back."

In the shower, Barbara wondered about her mother's reply. Now, where in the world could she have been? She was usually home waiting for her.

A little later, over breakfast, her question was answered.

"Vittorio asked me to have tea with him yesterday afternoon." Mrs. McAllister seemed to be buttering a roll with more than the usual care.

"He did? Without me?"

"He wanted to talk to me," Mrs. McAllister said deliberating, and Barbara instinctively braced herself.

"Darling, I'm afraid this will be a shock for you. Vittorio has been offered a permanent position here, in Cortina."

Barbara pushed her chair back from the table in utter disbelief.

"You mean not come back to New York with us? Just now, when even *he* thinks I'm ready for my Eighth Test? And how can I go into the Nationals without him? You must have told him it's impossible!" She became aware of the shrillness of her voice, and the look in her mother's face stopped her from saying more.

"Hear me out, Barbara. He hasn't accepted definitely yet. But try to look at it his way, for once. I think he really wants to stay." Then she added, speaking slowly and somewhat harshly, "Other people have their own lives to lead too, you know."

Barbara nodded and sat quietly, embarrassed by her outburst.

"He wanted to know how I thought you'd take it," her mother continued, her voice more patient. "Maybe I shouldn't tell you this, but I have a feeling he won't take the opportunity if he thinks you will let it affect your skating."

Barbara perked up. "He's always liked New York. And he certainly has plenty of pupils there!" But she knew, as soon as she had said it, that it was herself she was thinking of, not Vittorio.

"Yes, he has, but this *is* home for him. And now that he's had a taste of it, he's quite reluctant to leave again."

Mrs. McAllister got up from the table, then added, "We don't need to talk about it any more right now, but I want you to take plenty of time in thinking it through. And be very careful what you say to Vittorio when you see him later."

The morning was windy and cold, and Barbara tried hard to shake the numbness inside her as she whipped around the still empty rink. She stopped a moment to rub her arms and shoulders, still sore from the previous day's climb. I always thought I was in good physical condition, she reflected glumly. With a sigh, she pushed off and glided to her patch, barely nodding to a skater who had just arrived.

I didn't even get a chance to tell mother about yesterday, she brooded. The news about Vittorio knocked everything out of focus. How *could* he not want to go back to New York with me? Barbara skated an angry paragraph double three, much too fast to be truly accurate. I only came to Europe so I wouldn't have to change teachers! Whoa! She told herself, braking her skates as well as the rush of her thoughts. She shook her head in disgust at the prints she had made on the ice and at her own attitude. Following him to Italy was my bright idea, she reminded herself; he's not to blame for it. And what's more, I love it here too, so I can certainly understand how he feels.

She skated to the edge of the rink, unbuttoning her new Loden jacket, then threw it over the railing onto one of the empty benches. The morning was warming up, but it looked as though the sky would remain closed. Clouds stretched across most of the mountains, with only a few of the very highest peaks, sparkling white, resting above the moving mass of gray. There *is* a spell over this town, she thought, as her eyes skimmed the view. I can feel it too. Barbara roused herself, getting back to her practice.

Free-skating began, and Barbara was eager to do some jumping. She skated faster and faster, to build up speed. Taking off on her right foot, she spun around in a well-executed axel, but landed poorly and lost her balance. She was up in an instant stroking forward around the ice, ready to try again.

Coming toward her along the wooden walkway, Vittorio Bianchi smiled to see her hover, birdlike, nearly motionless in midair, then come out of the jump with perfect skill.

"Brava, Barbara," he said, skating up to her with a wide smile. "This is what I've been watching for in your free-skating. I sensed that it was growing . . . a new freedom, a new enthusiasm. It's just what you needed to balance the precision of your school figures."

Barbara nodded. "I know what you mean. I do feel

freer . . . less earth-bound." She laughed. "Everything around here seems to be striving upward, toward the summits." She raised her arms dramatically, then let them fall against her sides. "Of course, one does come down too! Did you see me a few moments ago?"

The joy of leaping had momentarily dispelled her gloom, yet now that Vittorio was with her, her mother's words came back vividly.

"I hear there is a possibility that I shall lose you as a coach."

Before replying, he took her hand and led her toward a bench. "I want to stay here, Barbara. I really would like to. There are so many young skaters here who have not had your advantages!"

"But I . . ."

"You don't really need me any more. You are ready for the test, and the Nationals too. There are any number of competent coaches who could take you the rest of the way."

Barbara got up defiantly. "Name one!" She felt at once rejected and proud that he had said she could go it alone.

"Well, I thought perhaps Kate Engstrom." He smiled slowly, pleased that she was accepting his challenge.

"How do you know she can take me? How do we know who else she is training?"

"I'll write to her today, and we'll wait for her reaction. Meanwhile," Vittorio's voice became more businesslike, "let's have a few more axels, before the public session begins. I want to show you why you fell coming out of your leap before."

97

When a jostling group of youngsters arrived a while later, Barbara and her coach walked off the ice together.

"Whatever the outcome of my decision," Vittorio began, and Barbara eyed him with skepticism, "I want to help you build your free-skating program for the Nationals. I've looked forward to that, and we still have enough time in Cortina to do at least the preliminary work."

Slowly she nodded in agreement, knowing then without a doubt that his decision had been made.

"We could start selecting some of the music after lunch." He watched her face for a sign of her usual vitality.

"All right, Vittorio. I'll be at your house by two-thirty." Barbara's voice had gone flat, and she continued, "I don't think I want to wait for Mother to pick me up. I'll take the bus back to the hotel right now."

Barbara found her mother sitting on the terrace which overlooked the tennis courts. Surprised to see her watching the game with intense concentration, Barbara found herself wondering: is this what she does when she's not busy with me? Does she enjoy other sports?

Mrs. McAllister looked up, startled to see her back early. "How did you get here, Barbara? I was just about to see whether it was time to pick you up."

"Oh, I decided to take the bus. I just had to get out of there." She gave her mother a quick peck on the cheek, then flopped into a chair next to her.

"Shall we take the rest of the morning off and do some shopping? We could walk into town: it doesn't take that much longer, and it would give you a break from driving.

There must be some things you'd like to bring back, and I really haven't left you much time for shopping."

Mrs. McAllister seemed happy at the suggestion. "Why, yes, I did think I'd get a few flowered kerchiefs for gifts. And I also considered one of those cut velvet bags we saw in the window of that elegant shop. But do we have enough time before you're due back at the rink?"

"I'm not going back there today. I'm meeting Vittorio at his house, and not until two-thirty, so we do have time for shopping. He thinks we should start work on selecting the music for my free-skating program," she continued, "and plan the moves I'll skate. That way I'll have his advice on using the steps I do best, and in New York my new coach can help me perfect the routine."

Even as she said it, Barbara knew that she could never keep Vittorio from what he really wanted to do, nor did she want to try. She knew, too, from the smile on her mother's face, that Mrs. McAllister was proud of her.

Barbara went on. "While we're in town, there's an album of mountain songs that I'd like to try to find."

"To take home with you, Barbie?"

"Well, yes, but mostly because there's one song I'd like to use in my routine. It's a slow, melancholy one. Good for my spirals and spread eagles. Now, what was it called?" She shrugged her shoulders. "I heard it that first day I went hiking with Fiammetta and Neil," she explained to her mother. "One of them will surely remember it, if I can't find it by myself."

Mrs. McAllister lightly tapped her forehead. "Neil! I almost forgot to tell you he called while you were at the rink. He was surprised to hear that you had felt up to skating so early this morning." She gave her daughter a quizzical look. "Am I wrong, or did something unpleasant happen yesterday? You don't have to tell me, Barbie, if you'd rather not."

At that point, Barbara was spared any further discussion by the sight of Dario, in tennis whites, crossing the terrace. In dismay, she realized he was coming toward her, and there was no way to avoid him. I thought I could put yesterday out of my mind, she thought furiously, and felt her cheeks turn hot.

The smile on his face was, she was sure, the most dazzling he could manage. He swept his racket aside and bowed low, and there, clutched over his heart, was the little bunch of edelweiss.

"Barbara, won't you please take these? I couldn't bring myself to give them to you yesterday, after they caused so much trouble. But I do want you to know that I'm sorry to have frightened you."

His posturing was melodramatic, but there was no mistaking his sincerity, and Barbara managed a half smile. She accepted the slightly wilted bouquet.

"Thank you, Dario. I'll keep them pressed in a book, as a memento."

The whole episode might seem very glamorous some day in retrospect, she thought. Dario included. But not right now, not yet!

She noticed that her mother had walked on ahead and seized the chance to end the conversation.

"I have to catch up with my mother now, Dario. I'll see you around!"

Barbara found *La Montanara*, the mountain song she liked, and Vittorio agreed that it would make a fine opening number for her free-skating program. For a change of pace, they decided she would then go into *The Rain in Spain* from *My Fair Lady*. They spent hours listening over and over to the many records Barbara had brought, finally selecting a group of pieces from opera and ballet. For the ending, both of them liked *I Feel Pretty*, an exuberant song from *West Side Story* that would allow her to express her newly found facility in leaping.

They timed and rerecorded the entire presentation on Vittorio's tape recorder, and then began the most exciting part of preparing a free-skating program: choreographing the skating moves.

For four minutes during the Nationals Barbara would be alone on the ice, expected to skate over the entire area of the rink with grace and originality as well as precision. The four minutes would flash by for the spectators, finished almost before the applause for the previous skater had died away. But before that moment, months of painstaking work lay ahead.

The long days of polishing and perfecting could wait until Barbara was back in New York. For the moment, she would rely on Vittorio's knowledge of her strengths and weaknesses. He would decide which moves should be included and which sifted out, and lay out the steps she would skate to each tune.

Early in the morning and late in the evening, and as often as it was possible to find the rink empty, Barbara experimented under Vittorio's watchful eye. Fiammetta, now that her contract with the Ice Revue was signed, had given up her job at the toy shop and was working alongside her friend, practicing her own routines.

It seemed that whenever the two girls sat down to rest, their conversation turned inevitably to the fact that Vittorio would not be there to help them when they reached New York.

"I heard about it the night before we went climbing," Fiammetta said, the first time they discussed it. "I kept thinking about it all through the day, wondering how you would feel, but my parents had warned me not to mention it. Vittorio wanted to discuss it with your mother first."

Barbara stirred her coke with a straw, her thoughts going back to that day which seemed to have brought her a new understanding.

"You could have made it very hard for him, you know," Fiammetta continued. "I think he would have gone back with you, had he felt that it would affect your skating career."

Barbara gave her friend a warm smile. "Well, I'll tell you something too. I'm awfully glad one of the Bianchis is coming back with me. This summer has brought so many new experiences, I'd hate to part with all of them!" She counted off on her fingers. "Your uncle is staying behind, and so are the mountains I've fallen in love with. Neil is going back to England at the end of the week. Thank heaven I'll have you to take home as a souvenir!"

"For me the new experiences are ahead, all just beginning!" Fiammetta looked radiantly happy. "By the way, what day *is* Neil leaving? I do want to see him before he goes."

As it turned out, Mrs. McAllister had invited all the Bianchis to have dinner at the hotel on the evening before Neil was due to leave for England. Barbara asked if he could join them, and it was, despite all the good-byes to come, a cheerful gathering of friends.

Neil's bus to Milan was an early morning one, so he was the first to excuse himself. Barbara walked him through the lobby to the front door of the hotel. She held her hand out to him, and he pulled her toward him.

"Come say good-bye to me outside?"

She nodded, feeling shy. He held the door open for her, then as she walked out into the crisp night air, she felt his arm lightly around her shoulder.

"We'll see each other again, you know," he said with assurance.

"Oh, I hope so!" she answered, not even trying to disguise the eagerness in her voice.

They took a few steps along the graveled path. Away from the lights of the hotel, Barbara could not see the expression on his face, yet it was no surprise to feel his cheek next to hers. Then his lips brushed hers very gently.

"I've always wanted to study architecture in the United States," his voice was a whisper, no louder than the rustle of the tree above them, "now I shall have added incentive to make my plan work."

She pressed her face against the rough texture of his jacket. Struggling to keep her voice steady, she murmured, half laughing, "We have marvelous modern buildings in New York!"

He pushed her firmly away from him, holding her by

the shoulders. "I'll make it happen, you'll see. And don't you be so busy skating that you forget to answer my letters!"

For a moment he held both her hands, then dropped them and walked away.

Chapter Twelve

There was little opportunity for Barbara to dwell on what she was leaving behind. All through the flight from Italy, mother and daughter answered a thousand questions from Fiammetta about life in the United States. Clothes, prices, subways and the theater, dating and what newspapers to read, slang expressions and even politics—all were discussed as the plane winged across the ocean. When the distant lights of New York City appeared, Fiammetta's English became tangled with Italian in her rush to express her wonder.

Delighted to be looking at New York through the eyes of a newcomer, Barbara resolved to spend most of her time sightseeing with Fiammetta during the few days they would have together. They were still planning the next day's itinerary when Mrs. McAllister unlocked the door to their apartment and the elevator man deposited their baggage on the living room floor.

Barbara took Fiammetta straight into the room they were to share, causing another burst of enthusiasm. Taking in the spacious, well-lit room, the handsome modern furniture, the glassed-in cabinet that displayed her trophies, Barbara had to admit it was good to be home.

Before they had time to unpack, the phone rang. Mrs. McAllister could be heard talking for a few moments before coming in to announce, "It's Kate Engstrom calling to welcome us home. She's already booked you for a skating lesson early tomorrow morning. Should I tell her you'd rather wait a few days before you start?"

Barbara hesitated. She wanted to share Fiammetta's journey of discovery, yet now she was eager to start work with the new coach who had so willingly taken her on.

"Do take your lesson, Barbara," Fiammetta urged, lifting one of the suitcases onto her bed. "I'm as anxious as you are to find out how you will like your new pro. And I have almost a week before I go to Chicago to join the ice show. We'll have time for sightseeing!"

Barbara was glad to pick up the phone and confirm the time of the session.

Fiammetta was still sleeping when Barbara awoke early the next morning. She tiptoed into the bathroom, carrying a skating outfit and the new Tyrolean sweater which Vittorio had given her as a going-away present. She set the table for breakfast while Mrs. McAllister scrambled eggs. Even in that old bathrobe, and without any makeup, Barbara thought, she looks well-rested and pretty. I hope the trip did her some good too.

"You know what, Mother? Don't bother getting dressed to drive me to Iceland. I can go alone. That way you'll have time to get settled and Fiammetta can sleep a little longer."

The pleased expression as her mother accepted reminded Barbara of an evening in Cortina when they had listened to one of the guests at the hotel describe a trip to Venice. A wistful look had come over Mrs. McAllister's face, and Barbara had impulsively blurted out, "Why don't we leave here three or four days early and spend some time in Venice? I really haven't given you a chance to be a tourist in Italy. . . ."

Mrs. McAllister had quickly refused, realizing the importance of the work Vittorio was doing with Barbara. There had been no further talk about it, just a pat on the hand and an appreciative smile. But the last few days in Italy had been happier and more relaxed for both mother and daughter.

A feeling of buoyancy and self-assurance came over Barbara as she rushed up the stairs to the rink, skates flung over her shoulder. She had wondered if she would hate the sight of Madison Square Garden without Vittorio puffing on his cigar, resplendent in a dark blue blazer. Yet she was immediately aware of Kate Engstrom waving to her in greeting.

Her new pro finished a conversation with one of the mothers, then came over with long, athletic strides. Barbara was reminded sharply of Marie Whitman, and how fond she had been of Kate. One of her coach's greatest assets, Marie had felt, was having been a champion so recently. All the aspects of training were still fresh in Kate's mind, she used to say. Barbara shook her head vigorously, as if to free her thoughts from ghosts.

"Well, how was your summer?" Miss Engstrom began in a brisk tone. "Vittorio wrote that you have been making great progress. How about getting out to your patch and letting me see what we have to work with?"

107

With that, the Italian interlude was truly over, and Barbara was back in the familiar rink. Anxious to impress her new coach, she was oblivious to the other skaters who were concentrating on their own efforts.

When she was finally ready to rest, she walked up the stairs to the coffee shop and ordered a second breakfast. Many of the boys and girls had spent the summer away, and there was much good-natured exchange of vacation news and progress reports from those who had continued their training. Kate came in and sat down with her newest pupil.

Through the glass enclosure Barbara had been watching a young woman rehearsing a one-foot spin.

"Miss Engstrom," Barbara wondered, "who is that directly below us? She seems familiar to me, yet I can't place her."

"You mean Vicky Weber? She hasn't been around in a couple of years."

"Didn't she place in the Nationals not too long ago?"

"Right. She came in third, two years ago. Then she got married and stopped competing."

"And now," Barbara wanted to know, "is she just skating for fun?"

"Oh, no, not at all. She came out of retirement shortly after the crash to help rebuild the team."

Vicky executed a split jump. Kate gave an approving nod and continued, "She's been at it all summer, and she's really pretty good now. At first everyone thought she'd be too rusty to ever catch up."

A strange sensation was sweeping over Barbara as their talk went on. Surprise? No, it couldn't be that, because she knew there had to be others training for the Nationals. Resentment? Against this girl she didn't even know? Surely it couldn't be easy to come back into a competitive sport after having left it all behind. Yet a combination of these feelings was at work in Barbara, and for several days she was too ill at ease to speak to Vicky.

Then, one afternoon, as she was about to call her mother from the booth at the side of the rink, the phone rang. She picked it up, and a male voice asked to speak to Mrs. Myers.

"I beg your pardon?" Barbara didn't know anyone at the rink by that name.

"Vicky Myers. Vicky Weber, I mean."

Barbara called Vicky off the ice, and sat down to wait until the booth was empty. When Vicky was finished, she came over to her.

"Thanks for paging me. I guess we haven't met yet, although I've been watching you skate the past few days. You're awfully good. Where have you been training?"

"I'm Barbara McAllister. I've been away all summer, working out with my pro in Italy. He stayed behind though," she continued, "and now I've switched to Kate Engstrom. It's hard at first, when you're starting with someone new." She hadn't meant to confide in Vicky, and she regretted the words immediately.

But Vicky understood. "Sure it is. I started with a new coach when I came out of retirement."

The phrase sounded funny to Barbara, coming from this smiling, brown-eyed girl, whose childish bangs and short straight hair made her seem no older than herself.

"Are you working toward the Nationals too?" Vicky wanted to know.

"Yes. But first I have to take the Eighth Test. Very soon. And what with classes starting next week, I feel really pressed for time. You're lucky you don't have school to worry about!" Barbara couldn't help relaxing with this friendly, outgoing girl.

"Well, maybe not school," Vicky didn't take her remark lightly, "but I have an apartment to take care of, laundry, marketing, cooking, and a husband who's not really sure he wants me back in skating."

In an instant Barbara saw just how many routine details her mother handled for her each day. In their household, everything revolved around her own skating ambitions. And to think that she had considered it a real contribution just to get herself to the rink the last few mornings!

"Did you say your husband doesn't like you to skate?" Strange, to be discussing marriage and responsibility. They seemed to belong to a different generation. Yet Vicky couldn't be more than three or four years older, and, as skaters, they held the same goals.

Vicky replied slowly. "Oh, he likes me to skate, all right. In fact, he enjoys joining me out on the ponds on week-ends."

That sounds pleasant, Barbara thought. A hazy picture of herself dancing on the ice with Neil flickered through her mind.

Vicky went on. "Don was very understanding, after we lost all our best skaters, when I felt I ought to come back and help rebuild the team."

And did she think she'd have a clear field, Barbara wondered. And use it as her chance to shine?

But if Vicky had any such hopes, she did not discuss them as she continued to explain her situation at home.

"Trouble is, he didn't realize how much of my time and energy would have to go into training. But if I'm going to compete at all, I have to put in at least as many hours as the kids who are working out all over the country. You're all younger, and you haven't lost two years, as I have."

"How do you know about the kids in training in other towns?" Barbara interrupted abruptly. In the back of her mind was a humiliating realization that it was perhaps only she who had expected a clear field.

"Well, a number of people got in touch with me about coming back into skating. And I asked a lot of questions about what my competition would be. After all, I wanted to make sure I had at least a fighting chance."

Vicky looked at Barbara with a questioning frown. "Much of this went on during the summer, while you were away," she went on. "Perhaps that's why you act so surprised. Just as well for you that you didn't know. I've heard that some skaters are purposely staying away from the better-known rinks to keep their free-skating routines a secret. And it makes me very nervous!"

Resolutely she got to her feet. "Which is why I'm going back to the salt mines right now!"

Barbara was left behind dumbfounded, irritated at her own naiveté. Well, there it is, she told herself. I could have found out all this just by asking Miss Engstrom, I suppose. But I don't find it easy to talk to her. Not like Vittorio.

. . . And anyway, I guess I must have wanted to fool myself by thinking there wouldn't be much competition. But I can't any more. Not after this conversation.

She squared her shoulders. I'll just have to skate that much harder, that's all.

The next day Fiammetta was due to leave for Chicago, and Barbara had suggested lunch in Chinatown before driving to the airport. Fiammetta, who had come to think she had experienced everything new and exciting that New York had to offer, was spellbound by the shops, the people and the food.

"How can I tell you how grateful I am?" she began, and to Barbara's astonishment, there were tears in her eyes. "I have felt truly like a member of the family since we have landed here. I wasn't sure how I would like being away from my family, but I know now that I have a home in America."

Mrs. McAllister reached across the table to squeeze her hand.

"We're counting on your being with us at Christmas when your show comes to New York," she said gently. "It will be just lovely, having two daughters instead of one."

With Fiammetta gone, Barbara went back to the tightly organized schedule which she always followed during the school year. She awoke early, skated, went to school, skated again in the afternoon, did her homework and went to bed, exhausted. Five days a week she kept to this routine; the only change the weekend brought was the fact that she skated even harder.

She was confident of her school figures. Even Miss Engstrom, who was not exactly free with compliments, said she didn't have much to worry about on that score. But the Eighth Test required free-skating, too, and that concerned her more.

Late one afternoon, while some of the skaters were already calling it a day, Barbara was practicing some complicated backward jumps. Miss Engstrom had been with her on the ice, studying each move and making frequent comments.

"I'm going home now, Barbara," she said, and her pupil came to a stop, sending up sprays of ice. "This jump needs a lot more than you've been giving it. It lacks spirit. In fact, your skating has been quite listless the last few days. Perhaps you've been overworking. You should try to relax more."

Her hand made a gesture of dismissal, unconscious, to be sure, but Barbara felt a chill that had nothing to do with the temperature.

She really doesn't care, Barbara thought. She can make a criticism like that, and then leave the rink without even showing me how to correct my mistake. Vittorio would never have done that!

She stood where her coach had left her. I wouldn't mind going home either, she thought. What a long day it's been! But how can I relax: there isn't much time to go before the gold test, and I've got to lick this!

She stroked backward, angrily, picking up speed for the jump. Suddenly, a sharp pain surged through her right leg, just above the boot, and before she knew it she found herself on the ground. An echoing thud told her someone else had fallen. Automatically, she got to her feet, only to collapse again.

"Oh, Barbara, what have I done to you! My skate must have cut you—you're bleeding!" Vicky Weber was on one knee, bending over her, a look of horror on her face.

A wave of dizziness swept over Barbara. "I didn't look, Vicky. I didn't look before I went backward. Are you hurt too?" She wondered how it felt to faint. She caught a glimpse of other people coming to help and briefly closed her eyes.

"I'm all right, just a bump." Vicky was up, brushing the ice from her costume. "Help Barbara to the bench. She's hurt."

Many hands reached out in her direction, and she felt herself propelled across the rink. She sank down on a bench as one of the pros came forward with a tourniquet and a first aid kit. The pain wouldn't stop.

"This won't do. It looks like a deep gash. We'd better get you to a doctor."

Barbara mustered the strength to say, "Could someone take me home? I'd rather see my own doctor."

"I'll take her." Vicky's voice was cool and efficient. "One of you call her mother to warn her."

They all helped her hobble to the elevator, and as she passed, Barbara was aware of a group of women standing by the railing.

She thought she heard someone say, "Well, that's one way to get rid of competition!"

Chapter Thirteen

*I*t's impossible! It's just impossible!" The words whirled over and over in her head, and Barbara dug her fingernails into the palms of her clenched hands. She was lying in her own bed, leg propped up, the pressure of her skating boot gone. The pain had eased by then, and she simply could not accept the doctor's verdict.

Not skate for at least six weeks! It was unthinkable! To be so close to the Eighth Test, to that gold medal she had worked for all these years . . . when would she ever be able to take it again? Tears rolled down her cheeks, and Barbara wiped them away angrily, rubbing her face into the pillow. Her rage was even more intense now than earlier on the ice, just after Miss Engstrom had left her.

Darn that Engstrom! Darn that Vicky! Why did she have to ram into me! I bet she did do it on purpose.

Her mind recalled the blurred vision of the women at rinkside and the whispered comment she had overheard.

No. She stopped herself. I know those mothers. Some are so jealous for their children that they'd say anything to hurt a better skater. No, it wasn't Vicky's fault. I'm the one who backed into her. And it all happened because I was so angry that I didn't look.

The door opened slowly, interrupting her bitter reflections.

"I'd hoped you might be sleeping," Mrs. McAllister said softly. She looked as though she were about to sit on Barbara's bed, then changed her mind and pulled up a chair instead.

"I just spoke to Miss Engstrom. She was terribly shocked to hear of the accident."

"Oh, sure! She was practically the cause of it!"

"Barbara! What are you saying?!"

"She made me so mad this afternoon, I didn't look behind me. And that's what did it!"

Indignant, Mrs. McAllister countered, "Now, Barbara! You've made up your mind not to like her! You're still looking for a carbon copy of Vittorio!" Her voice became more gentle. "I surely don't blame you for being upset—this comes at a very bad time, I know. But it *was* an accident, not anyone's fault."

Talking about it made Barbara want to cry again. "What did Engstrom say about postponing the test?" she asked, fighting off tears.

"She's getting in touch with the Figure Skating Association. She'll call us when there's a new date, she said. In any case, it can't be for six weeks."

Mrs. McAllister sighed, and repeated, "Six weeks . . . that's the longest you've gone without skating since you first started. . . ."

That six weeks was to seem longer than Barbara had imagined time could stretch. The first two weeks she was confined to bed, with occasional periods on the living room couch. She felt enveloped in gloom, couldn't think of anything except what she was missing. Reading might have taken her mind off her forced inactivity, but it held no appeal at all. The many books her mother brought lay around the room, and the December issue of *Skating,* when it came in the mail, only brought on renewed floods of tears.

After the stitches were removed, Barbara was able to return to school on crutches. Yet to be on her feet at all made her miss skating that much more. The same girl who had been so thrifty with her time that she could sweep through her homework in short, concentrated sessions, now sat with a book open on her lap for hours. She doodled in the margins of her physics problems, daydreamed over each composition, failed the first math test in her school career.

Her thoughts kept going back to the busy, eventful summer. Why didn't Neil keep his promise to write? She drafted a long letter to him, one bleak afternoon. In the end she tore it up, for it was so full of self-pity that she couldn't bear to have him read it.

When Kate Engstrom came to visit, they didn't seem to have anything to talk about. Kate felt they should get busy on planning a new costume for the coming competition. Barbara leafed through some sketches, fingered a few fabric samples her mother had collected, but all that came of it was a dispirited, "Well . . . I just don't know. . . ."

At the back of her mind was a fear that she could not bring herself to mention. It was Vicky who eventually uncovered it during one of her frequent calls on the Mc-Allisters.

"What did the doctor have to say when you saw him this morning?" she asked Barbara.

"Oh, the doctor. . . . I can't help wondering if he isn't just stringing me along. He keeps saying *at least* six weeks, and they're almost over. But how do I know it's not going to be longer?"

Barbara's face looked pale and thin, and her eyes were wide with the doubts she had been suppressing. "Suppose he just hasn't had the nerve to tell me that I'll never be able to skate again?"

Vicky got up quickly and put her arm around the younger girl's shoulders.

"Oh, Barbie! You've been brooding by yourself too long! I was there when the doctor first examined you: I saw his face. He couldn't have kept anything like this from all of us, knowing how your life centers on skating."

She walked over to the window, then turned. "I'll tell you what would be good for you. Come to the rink and watch us practice. . . ."

Barbara immediately shook her head, but Vicky wouldn't let her speak.

"It'll be hard the first few minutes, but at least you'll be where the pulse is. Right now you are much too isolated." She paused, and then said with a rush, "And Barbara, you'd be helping me, actually, if you showed your face at the rink."

Barbara at last showed some interest. "What do you mean, helping you?"

It was Vicky's turn to hesitate. "Well, perhaps I shouldn't say this, but there are a lot of people who think I hurt you on purpose, to get you out of my way."

Barbara nodded. "I remember the whispers right after the accident. I had hoped you hadn't heard."

Vicky shrugged. "Well, they're still at it. I've been getting a cold shoulder ever since."

"All right, Vicky." The voice was again strong, positive. "I'll come and watch you tomorrow. Whether it cheers me up or not, at least we'll silence the bench sitters!"

Barbara's entrance did not go unnoticed. As she hobbled off the elevator with Vicky Weber at her side, several ladies put down their knitting and came over to greet her. She found it awkward to answer their solicitous queries as to when she would be back on the ice, and to her relief, she soon heard Kate Engstrom's voice behind her.

"Better come and sit down, Barbara." Kate sounded most authoritative. "No sense putting too much strain on your leg."

Kate's smile was warm and welcoming as she found room for Barbara on one of the benches, then made herself comfortable beside her.

Vicky slipped off her sweater and gave it to Barbara to hold.

"Do me a favor?" Her voice was loud enough for all to hear. "Watch my forward bracket turn. I know it could be smoother, but I can't quite figure out how to improve it."

"Okay, Vicky. Let me see if I can help." Barbara gave her a wink, and Vicky was off.

"What are you girls up to?" Kate Engstrom tilted her head to one side. "Oh, never mind, I think I know. I'm glad you've talked it out. And I'm glad you came down here, Barbara."

Her pupil glanced left and right. "It feels odd being a spectator. I should have brought my knitting, I guess."

Kate laughed. "Hoorah! Your sense of humor isn't altogether dead. I must say, you had me worried the last few times I came to see you—so down-in-the-dumps all the time."

Barbara shifted in her seat, embarrassed.

"It won't be long now before you're back on skates," Kate continued, "and we'll need all the vitality you can muster to make up the time we've lost."

Somehow, that "we" made Barbara sit up straighter. Is she treating me differently, she wondered, or am I the one who is thawing out?

A few days before Christmas the doctor told her to throw away her crutches. He prescribed whirlpool treatments to strengthen her muscles, a series of exercises to be followed faithfully, and told her to go back to skating half an hour a day. She was to build up to her regular routine gradually, he had emphasized, and she was not to overdo. Barbara accepted his limitations without argument, overjoyed at the prospect of being released.

It was snowing when the McAllisters left the doctor's office, and Barbara felt shaky. Still, she refused her mother's arm, and tried hard to walk without favoring her weaker leg.

As they came back to their apartment, they found a telegram under the door.

"It's from Fiammetta," Mrs. McAllister said smiling to her daughter. "The whole ice show company is arriving in New York tomorrow."

She set the message on the coffee table and looked around the room, then went on, "She wasn't due until

Christmas Eve. I'll be glad to see her, but my, I have a lot to do in the next few days."

Barbara gave her a happy hug. "Don't worry, I'll help you with everything! I didn't feel very festive before, but now I'm looking forward to all the preparations. We'll get some holly, and poinsettias, and some new ornaments, and we'll really show Fiammetta an American Christmas!"

She sat down and stretched her leg on the couch to rest it. Almost immediately, the doorbell rang, and the elevator man handed Mrs. McAllister a package.

"It's for you, Barbie. Ah, ha! A British stamp!"

"Oh, Mother!" Barbara tore at the brown wrapping paper, feeling a blush come to her cheeks. "You don't suppose it's . . ."

And it was, a present from Neil.

"Dear Champ," the note read, "I hope this will make you forgive my not writing. Read it through, and let me know if you'll have a go at Mt. Everest with me. Happy Christmas. Neil."

Barbara threw his card up into the air. She flopped contentedly the full length of the sofa, holding the book out for her mother to see.

" 'The Conquest of Everest'," Mrs. McAllister read in puzzlement. "Now, why would he send you that?"

Barbara hugged the book, a delighted smile on her lips.

"Oh, it's exactly what he'd send! And a perfect cure for Eighth Test jitters!"

Chapter Fourteen

A large area of the rink had been sectioned off for tests. No music played, and a sign lettered "Silence Please" was propped up on the ice near the three judges. Barbara stood stiffly between Kate Engstrom and her mother, trying to focus her attention on the red-haired boy executing a figure three.

She shivered. It was the first outward sign of apprehension Barbara had shown, and Kate put an arm firmly around her pupil.

"Did you sleep well last night?" Miss Engstrom's voice was hushed.

"Very well, thank you, but I woke up awfully early. On the one day when I could have slept longer!"

Barbara's eyes traced the moves of the boy taking the Second Test. He came to a stop, having finished a left backward inside circle eight, and she heard him say, "May I get a Kleenex from my father, please?"

The judge nearest to him, an elderly lady with tightly curled gray hair and glasses hanging from a strap around her neck, pulled a tissue from the pocket of her fur coat.

"Let's try not to have any more interruptions," she said coolly.

Barbara smiled at the abashed look on his face, then turned, hearing her mother speak to someone.

"As if he didn't have enough trouble skating backward, now he has to have a leaky nose too," the man at Mrs. McAllister's side was saying, half in worry, half in jest.

"The Second Test is hard for everyone," Barbara's mother reassured him. "But eventually, you'll see, it'll be as easy for him to go backward as forward."

"You're remarkably calm. I don't know how you can take it, watching your kid take test after test. . . ."

Barbara winced. Calm? Her mother was no more confident than she. Since the accident, Barbara had worked so hard to strengthen the injured leg that not enough time had gone into her school figures. Before her luck changed, she had felt ready for the test, but now. . . .

She saw the boy tiptoeing toward them. His father held out a duffel coat and helped him into it. Meanwhile, the judges were walking around his tracings on the ice, peering at them closely. One of them was down on his knees, his camel's-hair coat trailing behind. He made a notation on the clip board in his hand, then got up and walked off with the two ladies to compare their final scores.

Throughout this period, a girl Barbara knew was practicing at the very edge of the rink, lips pursed in concentration, long black braids swinging behind her. Barbara removed her skate guards and went over to join her. Better to work out for a while than to stand around and stew, she decided.

She proceeded to review the Eighth Test figures step by step, in the order required by the rule book. She was on her first paragraph loop when she noticed Kate near the railing, describing the same moves with her own body. Barbara smiled, and Kate beckoned to her.

"Watch yourself, Barbara. You were close to flatting that time."

Barbara nodded. Both edges of the skate blade had touched the ice simultaneously, if only for a few seconds. "I just noticed the tracings. Oh, Kate! Don't tell me I'm going to do that in front of the judges!"

Kate put a reassuring hand on her arm. "No, you won't. You just haven't warmed up yet, that's all. You have at least another hour to go, with Alice just coming to her turn now."

The judges were back at their places, and the younger girl zoomed over to them. Barbara watched Alice throw a dazzling smile at the youngest of the officials. The stately woman in the oversized fox hat replied with a stare that reverberated as far as Barbara.

"Brrr! That Mrs. Wilson. She judged some of my early tests, and she terrifies me!"

"That's just her public stance, Barbara. She's impeccably fair, you know that, and since her own skating days, she's helped any number of youngsters." In a no-nonsense tone, Kate continued, "Get back to work now, while I can still give you some pointers."

Barbara obeyed, knowing that, once her turn came, no one would be allowed to communicate with her.

Returning to her patch, she passed the red-haired boy and his father on their way to the exit. The satisfied smiles on their faces left no doubt as to the verdict of the judges.

"Congratulations!" Barbara whispered, wishing she were hearing those very words herself.

The hour flew by in concentrated practice, and all at once she realized that the judges had disappeared and that Alice was sitting on the bench next to her coach, twisting a handkerchief in her fingers.

A queasy feeling came over Barbara: she was next. Better take a break for a few moments.

One of the judges motioned to Alice and her coach, and they followed down the hall past the elevators.

"Did she do all right?" Barbara asked her mother. Skeptically, Mrs. McAllister looked at Kate. The coach spread her hands in doubt.

Moments later, Alice's pro sat down beside them looking grim.

"She's crying her eyes out in the bathroom. There's not a thing I can do for her there!"

"Is it the first time she's failed a test?" Mrs. McAllister asked.

"Yes, it is," he nodded. "The poor kid worked so hard on her free-skating, and now she won't even get to that part of the test. I was afraid she wasn't putting enough time into compulsory figures. . . ."

Barbara remembered how exciting it had been to work up her first free-skating program for the Sixth Test. She also recalled the time she had failed and how sharp the pain had been.

She saw the white-haired judge, galoshes flopping, coming in their direction, and she stiffened.

"Miss Engstrom," the official said, "we're going upstairs for a cup of coffee. We'll take on your girl in about fifteen minutes."

Barbara got quickly to her feet. "I'd just as soon keep

busy then. I think I'll go and see if I can talk to Alice. I don't know her very well, but I do know how she must feel." I had never even met Marie, she recalled, when she helped me get over my disappointment.

At the door to the bathroom Barbara called softly, "Alice?"

"Please go away. I don't want to see anyone!" The voice was muffled and shaky.

"It's Barbara. I wish you'd let me talk to you. . . ."

When they emerged together some minutes later, the judges were just filing in. Barbara gave her mother a quick peck on the cheek and squeezed the hand Kate Engstrom held out to her. One tug at the zipper of her practice outfit and she was on the ice.

She looked toward the extreme left-hand area of the rink; it had always been her favorite spot. Relieved to see that it was free of other markings, she tiptoed over, careful to preserve the surface on her way. The sound of the ice guards on the judges' boots followed her with a steady click-click.

She stopped and waited while the judges put fresh paper into their clip boards. When her eyes met theirs, she was ready too. She stretched her arms out wide, indicating the major axis, the line on which the centers of her circles would fall. The judges now separated and stood at different spots along her projected path. The test, which to a skater is the equivalent of a Ph.D., had officially begun.

With one clean single stroke from the outside edge of her right foot, Barbara moved forward into her first paragraph double three. She repeated it three times without pausing, then moved away while the judges checked her prints. Next came the same figure on the left foot. While the three judges marked their paper, she searched the surrounding ice for a clean place without glare on which to continue.

At the end of the first four figures, Barbara exhaled deeply, knowing things had gone well. The tracings told her there were no wobbles; nothing looked lopsided. And the next figure, the paragraph loop, was one whose challenge she had always enjoyed. She pushed off with her right foot and was startled to hear a voice immediately interrupt her.

"Make a fresh start. You didn't wait for the go-ahead."

Distressed, Barbara prepared to begin anew. That didn't count, she thought. But from here on, they'll deduct points. Remember: head erect . . . palms parallel to the ice . . . keep your free leg slightly bent. She was gliding. As she brought her non-skating leg ahead, smoothly extending her knee and ankle, a twinge in the injured tendon made her stiffen momentarily. Her graceful carriage was resumed in a second, but Barbara was too much a skater not to realize that her tension would be penalized.

Forget it, forget it, she told herself. Nobody ever makes six . . . that's perfection. She skated the rest of her paragraph loops with a determination unequaled in all her past years.

As the judges checked the last completed group of prints, she tried to keep herself from watching them. She was polishing up the next figure on a patch nearby when she caught sight of the white-haired judge crouching on the ice, comparing the size of the loop heads with her pencil. Why is she doing that, Barbara worried. Did I make one smaller than the other two? Are they all too small? The answer would have to wait.

Then they were ready for her to start on the last group of figures, the paragraph bracket. Toward the middle, she noticed that one of her changes of edge was longer than the length of her skate blade. That was no good, she reprimanded herself. I'd better correct it in the next two tracings or I'll flunk.

Flunk, fail, flop . . . how come they all start with F? Sitting on the bench while the judges were out computing her final score, Barbara found it easier to play with words in her mind than to make small talk with Kate and her mother. So much depends on my passing this test, she brooded. If I had failed when it was first scheduled, there would have been time to take it over before the Nationals. But not now. Now, if I fail, a whole year is shot.

She wiped the ice off her skate blades, looked up hopefully toward the corridor. Still no sign of the High Executioners. The skates felt tight, and she loosened the laces. More waiting. May as well put on my skate guards, she thought, noticing how moist her hands were. Her mother gently pushed a strand of hair back from her face.

"Barbara McAllister!"

Three heads turned as her name was called. Kate put a hand under Barbara's elbow, and they rose together. As she walked toward the judges, she couldn't read their faces at all.

"Congratulations, Barbara. You passed your school figures." Mrs. Wilson finally smiled.

Barbara flung herself at Kate and whirled her down the corridor.

"Whoa, Barbara! Hold it!" The words were stern, but the voice revealed Kate's own pleasure. "Don't you want to wait to hear your score?"

It was not the highest score Barbara had ever attained, but it didn't seem to matter, she reflected later, as she changed outfits for the free-skating part of the test. Although in the past, she might well have been disappointed not to have come up to expectations.

Barbara felt the judges must have known her leg bothered her. She only hoped she could forget the injury during the session to come next.

During the last part of the test, nothing got in the way of her success. Barbara whirled, glided, spun, jumped with a freedom and an enthusiasm she had not felt since her days in the mountains. There was no longer any tension, or fear that she might not pass. Only the sheer joy of skating, and intense gratitude that she was able to express herself in this way.

This glow carried her through the weeks that preceded the National Championships. There were, of course, moments of painful weariness and dull repetition. But the knowledge that she was ready to compete for the United States title crystallized all her efforts.

On the final evening of the United States Ladies Figure Skating Championship, an overcrowded taxi delivered Barbara to the Skating Club of Boston. Mrs. McAllister emerged first, arm held high, keeping her daughter's new costume away from the splatters of a muddy street. Next came Kate Engstrom, clutching Barbara's program record. Barbara jumped out, then reached carefully for her freshly polished skates and the little suitcase that held everything she would need.

"Here! Let me take that!" Fiammetta was last to get out of the cab and followed the entourage into the building.

Barbara slipped her free arm through her friend's. "I'm so happy you managed to be here tonight! I had hoped to see you yesterday, too, but I guess one day was all you could take off, huh?"

Fiammetta nodded. "Your mother told me at the station how close the scores were yesterday, on the compulsory figures."

"Yes, we seem to be pretty even on that level," Barbara replied. "Someone will really have to shine tonight."

She pushed open the door of the dressing room to a flurry of talk and giggles. Like splashes of primary color on an artist's palette, the skaters bustled through their preparations in bright new program dresses.

One stood, statue-like, while her mother sewed up a split seam. Another grimaced into the mirror, dissatisfied with the effect of her first try at lipstick. Several made gingerly attempts at combing their hair, afraid to destroy the afternoon's settings. Propped up on benches and shelves sat an assortment of dolls, stuffed animals and trolls, bearers of good fortune to their nervous owners.

Barbara caught sight of Vicky Weber, alone in one corner, engrossed in a series of deep knee bends. She made her way to her side, and Vicky smiled to see her.

"I was getting worried you might be late. Two cables came for you when I first got here. Oh! Barbara! I'm so nervous! It's been so long since I've been in a competition!"

Barbara introduced her to Fiammetta as she tore the cablegrams open. The first was from Vittorio. She longed to have him there, backing her up, lending the comfort of his friendship. But that thought was quickly dispelled by the excitement of hearing from Neil.

"Hurry up and get dressed, Barbara!" her mother urged as she was handed the message from Vittorio. The anxious edge in her voice made Barbara decide that she would save Neil's wire for a more private moment. She slipped it into her suitcase.

"I guess we don't have to ask who the second cable is from," Fiammetta laughed as she helped Barbara zip up her gentian blue costume. She gave the chiffon skirt a final fluffing to make sure it would fall right, then took Mrs. Mc-Allister's hand.

"Why don't you and I leave now and go find our seats? Miss Engstrom will take care of anything Barbara may need."

Mrs. McAllister hesitated. "Are you sure I ought to leave you, Barbie?"

Barbara kissed her on the cheek. "The warm-up period will begin any second, so you may as well go and sit down. Just keep those fingers crossed, both of you!"

The audience applauded warmly when they all came out together. They know how nervous we all are, Barbara thought, moving in long, graceful strokes over the entire surface of the rink. Besides the family and friends of the evening's competitors, the stands included all the skaters involved in other events: pairs, junior and senior men, junior ladies and dance teams. Barbara tried to identify her mother and Fiammetta, but all she could see was a blur of faces.

A few moments later, the ice had been cleared and the skaters were back in the dressing room, awaiting the announcement of names over the loudspeaker.

"Oh," sighed Vicky, "I'm glad I'm not first to go on. That Colorado girl looked white as a ghost when she was called."

Barbara nodded. "I must say, though, that I was glad my name was drawn among the early ones. With the lots picked as they were, you're going to have an awfully long wait."

Vicky sat silently for a while, nose buried in a gardenia which she held in her hand.

"Were you able to eat anything?" she said suddenly. "My husband had a steak sent up to the hotel room but I couldn't even look at it!"

"I picked at a T-bone and managed to get down a glass of milk. I felt I really ought to have at least that." Barbara hugged her Tyrolean sweater tightly around her.

"You cold?" Vicky edged closer to her on the bench.

Barbara grinned. "Yes. But also, I hope the sweater brings me luck. My ex-coach gave it to me."

"Don gave me the gardenia for luck," Vicky said smiling. "I guess he just doesn't think like a skater, or he'd know we can't take a chance on wearing something that might fly off!"

Barbara sprang up. "That reminds me! I'd better check my head band and make sure *it* stays on." She walked across the room, continuing over her shoulder, "I don't usually wear this kind of thing, but mother and Kate both liked the idea of something sparkling in my hair."

Vicky's comment was lost to her as she stood before the

mirror because one of the skaters, a finalist from the Mid-West, burst into the dressing room, commenting loudly to one of her friends, ". . . and then as she came out of a mazurka jump, she fell! You should have heard the audience groan! You'd think she'd tried something really difficult!"

Barbara turned away abruptly and walked back to Vicky, frowning.

"Ugh! I can't stand dressing room gossip!"

Vicky agreed. "I also don't understand how some people can go up there and watch another skater's program. . . ."

"It would make me doubt my own routine. I never do it!"

"Of course it's different for the two of us. We've become so familiar with each other's material. . . ." Vicky placed her gardenia back in its box, and went on, almost to herself, "To tell you the truth, I don't really know how I feel about being back in competitive life. At first, I thought only of helping to rebuild the team. But now that I've made the comeback, I'm out to win tonight. Still . . . it'll make for problems at home, no matter how it turns out. . . ."

She looked Barbara full in the face. "It's quite different for you, I know."

The words "win tonight" had lit up in Barbara's mind like a flash bulb. She saw herself surrounded by photographers and reporters, cradling a trophy in her arms. Enough of that, she scolded herself.

She held up her hands and crossed her fingers, turning to Vicky. "Here's to both of us, anyway."

A silence had enveloped the dressing room as more

names were called and the number of girls dwindled. Some sat and stared at the floor, others snuggled deeper into their coats.

Barbara checked her boot laces for the hundredth time.

She knew the best skating talents available in the country were vying for the national title. She was one of them, she knew that too. And if tonight she didn't come in first, there would be other times. All the years of training, of single-minded devotion to one goal, had brought her this far. Then, why the nervousness?

The loudspeaker crackled and now the name she heard was her own.

Vicky tapped her lightly on the shoulder, and Barbara left the dressing room. At the rink railing, Kate Engstrom was waiting. She took the skate guards as Barbara removed them, then helped her off with her sweater.

Hands on the rail, Barbara executed a few warm-up pliés. In one elegant streak, she was at the center of the rink. For endless moments, she stood and waited, imprisoned by a frozen beam of spotlight. Then the first bars of her mountain song set her free.